"I'm here to make sure you don't screw up."

"Thank you." She pressed her forehead to his. "But... you and me. *That* could screw things up. For me."

With no words to make his case, he kept quiet, because she was right. More than she could have known. In his current condition, he'd ruin her. Just drag her down into the dark depths with him.

All her optimism and exuberance would be gone. And that would kill him.

"Unless it's just one more time."

Again, he thought perhaps words were going to get in his way at this point. Especially when he liked where this was headed.

"Sam?"

Great, now he was going to have to say something that might possibly risk this. "Right there with you."

"So, you agree? One more time? Just to see if—"

"If it was a fluke."

"Right. Because maybe it was that night, or the mojitos, or the city, or the fact that we were both lonely."

He knew it was none of those things. Not for him. "Sure. We could tell ourselves that."

"Or we could find out. For sure."

* * *

WELCOME TO WILDFIRE RIDGE!

Dear Reader,

Welcome to Wildfire Ridge and the romance between two soul mates who might have never seen each other again after one special night. But fate, or kismet, whichever you prefer, intervenes and throws these two together again.

Jill is a secondary character from *This Baby Business*, so engaging and entertaining that I knew I'd have to tell her story. I love writing about strong women, and Jill Davis is just that. She's the CEO of her own company, confident and capable. But when her one-night stand shows up to work for her company, she's not certain how to react. She'll never turn away a military man in need of a job, but it's going to be a challenge to be around Sam and keep it professional.

Sam Hawker is a former US marine in need of a job, but he's surprised to find his boss is the woman who got him through a very difficult time based on the memory of one single night. Because Sam needs far more than a job, even if he won't admit it.

I hope you enjoy this first book in the Wildfire Ridge series as much as I enjoyed writing it.

Heatherly Bell

More than One Night

Heatherly Bell

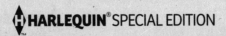
HARLEQUIN SPECIAL EDITION

Recycling programs
for this product may
not exist in your area.

ISBN-13: 978-1-335-57399-5

More than One Night

Copyright © 2019 by Maria F. Buscher

Printed in U.S.A.

Heatherly Bell tackled her first book in 2004 and now the characters that occupy her mind refuse to leave until she writes them a book. She loves all music but confines singing to the shower these days. Heatherly lives in Northern California with her family, including two beagles—one who can say hello and the other a princess who can feel a pea through several pillows.

Books by Heatherly Bell

Harlequin Special Edition

Wildfire Ridge

More than One Night

Harlequin Superromance

Heroes of Fortune Valley

Breaking Emily's Rules
Airman to the Rescue
This Baby Business

Other titles by Heatherly Bell
are available in ebook format.

To
Sergeant David Mock, USAF, WWII 1943–1946
and
Tim Buscher

Chapter One

Note to self: should you ever again decide to hang the American flag on a rusty old pole, do not wear shorts when doing so. Definitely going on her long list of "Things to Never Do Again."

Stuck. She was 100 percent stuck. Story of her life.

Jill Davis clung to the metal pole on which she'd hung the flag, eyeing the ladder that had toppled to the ground with a mixture of longing and plain old disgust. Her legs were wrapped tightly around the pole, her arms clinging like it was the last box of shoes on clearance at Macy's.

It was a beautiful late spring day in Fortune, California, the sun shining brightly, the temperature in the mild and comfortable midseventies. Hence the shorts, which had seemed like a good idea at the time. Not so much now.

She could shimmy down the pole, but she'd likely cut up her inner thighs doing so. Someone would come along soon. She was almost sure of it. Her new employees would be showing up in a couple of hours. Big, strong and brawny veterans from Home at Last, the nonprofit veterans employment placement agency. She had a lot of work ahead for them if she ever expected to get Wildfire Ridge's Outdoor Adventures ready to open in a month's time.

She should have probably waited for them to show up and had one of them raise the flag. That would have made sense. Instead, she'd had the grand idea that she wanted them to enter onto the grounds of Wildfire Ridge and be welcomed at once by the majestic American flag.

And now she was stuck.

At first, she heard only a deep rumbling sound in the distance. But when Jill turned, from her unique bird's-eye view she caught a puff of dust kicked up by a motorcycle headed up the small dry dirt road that led to their entrance. Salvation in the form of a Hell's Angel? No matter, she'd take it. Jill blew out a breath. She was probably going to look a little silly up here. But hey, it wouldn't be the first time in her life she'd been left hanging. See? She still had her sense of humor intact.

The motorcycle was definitely headed her way, picking up speed as it rounded the curve. She hadn't expected any of the four men to arrive for a couple of hours, so this might be someone else entirely. Someone curious about Wildfire Ridge. Ever since she'd been dealing with the city council, and the various hoops they made her jump through on a regular basis, curious residents would drive up the hill known for wildfires from time to time to see how much progress she'd made.

This motorcycle rider, he or she, was probably a bit of an adrenaline junkie, being that they rode a motorcycle. Her perfect client. When the place was open and running, they'd be providing plenty of extreme sports and activities for the Silicon Valley set.

The motorcycle slowed and the rider's helmet tipped up, seemingly to take in the view. Now Jill could see that the rider was definitely a man. He was built like a running back, tall, with long legs that slid from the motorcycle after he shut it off. The scuffed black leather boots he wore thudded against the hard ground. He still wore his helmet so she couldn't get a good look at his face. Even so, she heard the smile in his voice.

"Hey...what's up?"

"That's *funny*. Would you mind giving me a hand, please?"

It only took him a second to right the ladder and place it close to the pole. He held it steady with both hands while she reached for it and made her way down one rung at a time. She felt a little self-conscious the closer she got to him, as she realized that from his position he was getting a real good look at her bottom. Not to mention her bare legs. Good thing she regularly tortured herself at the gym. But as soon as she got Outdoor Adventures open, she was going to do all the fun kinds of exercises like hiking and zip-lining, along with everyone else.

Anyway, what should she care what this guy thought of her butt? She couldn't answer that, except for the fact that she liked the way he walked. There was something so familiar about it and... Dare she say it? *Sexy*. Unfortunately, that was probably more of a testament to the fact that she'd been celibate for three years, so every man was beginning to look good to her. Even this easy rider dude.

He still hadn't taken that damned helmet off, which gave him a bit of a storm trooper look. On second thought, more of a Darth Vader look, seeing that he was dressed all in black. The only thing missing was the cape.

If he started to sound raspy and out of breath, she was going to scream.

On the last rung, she turned to thank Darth Vader. "I really appreciate this."

"What the hell? Angelina?" He pulled his helmet off to reveal a gorgeous head of dark blond hair and a set of bright blue eyes she'd never managed to forget.

"Chris?"

He grinned, slow and easy. "My real name is Sam."

For a moment, Jill couldn't take in a breath. Her *Chris.* She'd given him that name and asked him to call her *Angelina.* Her one-and-only one-night stand from three years ago. San Francisco. Too many mojitos. A Marine on leave. Jill, far too patriotic for her own good. One night. It wasn't supposed to follow her into her carefully arranged life. She coughed, a choking sound.

He squinted. "Are you okay there?"

She didn't speak for a moment, simply nodded. "My real name is Jill."

"I'm going to guess that you're Jill Davis, owner of Wildfire Ridge's Outdoor Adventures."

Jill found her voice, weak as it sounded to her now. "And you must be Sam Hawker, my new employee."

Thirty minutes later, Jill had "Chris," aka Sam Hawker, in her office trailer filling out paperwork. W-2 forms, emergency contact forms. As he straddled the chair, she flashed back to the night three years ago, when she'd straddled him.

Oh boy.

Humiliating. The only time she'd ever taken such a huge risk with a guy, and now she had to be his boss. She wasn't sure how this could work, unless she put some parameters in place. No way would she turn a Marine in need of a job away. But if they were going to be working together and getting this place into shape, they were going to have to forget... Something.

"Um...want some coffee?"

He glanced up, his lips twitching into a smile. "Sure."

"How do you like it?" She'd had wild monkey sex with the man and didn't know how he liked his coffee.

So wrong.

"Hot."

Well, she could have guessed that. She poured him a mug of black coffee and set it down next to him. He slid over his emergency contact form, blank. "There's no emergency contact."

"Why not? That's usually where you put in family. Like a...spouse or significant other." She slid it back to him.

"Nope." He slid it back. "No spouse. No significant other."

"What about parents? You have those?"

"Yeah. They're not my emergency contacts."

In-te-res-ting. The tone in his voice told her it was a subject best left for another lifetime.

"What should I do if something happens to you?"

"Nothing's going to happen to me. I'm apparently hard to kill."

She swallowed hard and pointed to the form. "I think I need to put something here."

"Call 911 if something happens." He lifted a shoulder.

"Okay." She made a note, feeling silly. Of course she'd call 911. But wasn't there anyone who'd care to know if he was hurt?

He took a gulp of his coffee and set it down, then stretched his arms out and she nearly drooled as muscles bunched up under his black tee. She had a distinct memory of those muscles. *Muscle memory.* That was a thing, she understood, just not the way she was thinking about it.

She cleared her throat. "I think we need to talk about it."

He set his pen down and leaned back, those deep blue eyes studying her. "Might be best."

"I mean, we're grown-ups here. Nothing to be ashamed of, yada yada."

"Agreed."

"But if we're going to be working together... I'm your boss. So we should talk about how *that's* never going to happen again."

"Huh."

"What does that mean? Is that a 'yes' huh, as in you agree?"

"With the way you've been staring at my ass, I thought you were going to go another way with that."

"I have not been staring at your...butt!"

"A little bit." He held his finger and thumb about an inch apart and sent her an easy smile.

"Okay, fine! But no more than you've been staring at mine."

"I won't deny it."

"Let me see if I can explain this to you. Do you know those bands that have one big hit and you never hear from them again? Kind of like all they had in them was one really fantastic song. And then—*poof*! That was the end of it."

"I see where you're going with this."

"We're a one-hit wonder."

"I'm going to have to disagree with you there. What you're forgetting is that a lot of the time those bands keep playing their music for their true fans. Great songs. Maybe no more hits because no one else hears about it. But believe me, their fans are enjoying the music."

Her face flushed. "I can't enjoy your…music. Not any-more."

"If that's how you want it."

"That's how it has to be." She picked up a set of keys. "You can finish the paperwork later. Let me show you to your trailer."

He picked up his duffel bag and followed her out the door. She led him to the section of live-in housing trailers she'd set up for the men. Unlocking the trailer, she climbed up the few steps.

"This is the biggest trailer. Might as well give it to you since you got here first. As you know, all you men have housing while we get the park ready to open. Meals included. You should have everything you need in here. If you need anything else, let me know. I'm in the office all day and even some nights." She took a breath. "By the way, I wanted the flag to be flying when you all arrived."

He quirked a brow. "Thanks."

"Okay." She moved to the door, ready to go. "You just get settled. We'll have our first meeting tomorrow morning bright and early."

She'd no sooner shut the door and headed down the steps than he opened it again. "Hey."

"Yeah?"

"What do you I call you? Jill? Boss? Ms. Davis? Angelina?"

"Jill is fine."

"Jill, thanks for the job."

And with that he shut his door.

Chapter Two

Sam Hawker might be a man of few words, and granted, he was often at a loss for them around beautiful women, but today? He had a few: *dayum*, for starters. Angelina's real name was Jill; she was now his boss; and how the hell did he get so lucky?

She smiled and then she was off, those long legs walking in the direction of her office trailer.

He shut his trailer door and took another look at his surroundings. This trailer with a small kitchen, wood cabinets and table, bathroom and cot in the back was more than he needed.

When he'd been hired through Home at Last to work for a woman named Jill who needed experienced hikers and guides for her outdoor adventure company, it sounded like the perfect job for him. The organization was an employment agency but because it focused solely on hiring veterans, Sam couldn't shake the feeling it felt like more "thanks for a job well done." He'd had enough thanks from well-meaning civilians. But since leaving the Marine Corps, he'd had trouble holding down a job. He'd dabbled in construction, done some roofing and a little welding. Nothing steady. He'd been feeling a little self-destructive for a time, searching for the hardest physical challenge possible, to make him feel accomplished. And nothing ever seemed physically punishing enough.

Just when he'd begun to wonder if he'd ever adjust to civilian life again and lead a normal life, this job had come up through the agency. The owner and operator wanted guides to take groups of clients on challenging hikes, zip-lining, rock climbing and wakeboarding at the lake. Sounded like a paid vacation to Sam.

He'd never expected, nor could he have expected, to run into the one woman who'd managed to get him through some of the roughest times of his life, both during and after deployments. Nights when he didn't care whether he lived or died.

She just didn't know it, nor would she ever. But he *remembered* her.

Unfortunately for him, far too well for a woman who would now be his boss. He had a distinct memory of the way she tasted, sweet and juicy as a peach in September. Of the way she'd moved in a steady and pulsating rhythm with him all night, not missing a beat, as if she, too, couldn't get enough. Couldn't go fast enough or hard enough. She'd given him the single most erotic night of his life.

And now she was his boss.

Late that afternoon, after the rest of her employees had been checked in and filled out their paperwork, Jill took a break from permits and W-2s and occasionally staring at Sam's butt. She drove the short distance into town to meet her two best friends, Carly and Zoey, at The Drip. A few years ago, all three of them had worked at the coffee shop together, enjoying three o'clock dance-offs and plenty of gossip. But now Zoey had taken over her aunt's pet store. Pimp Your Pet was doing well these days, and Zoey was rarely away from the store or a pet. Right now, her large rescue, Boo, a Great Dane, sat like a horse just outside The Drip. He had the patience of a Saint Bernard.

Carly had sold her mother's baby supplies and clothing company last year and now worked at home designing baby clothes. She was married to the walking Viagra for women, local pilot Levi Lambert. The angel currently bouncing on her knee was his baby daughter, Grace.

Jill had only stopped working the occasional shift here two months ago when all the funding had gone through for the park. She had several investors that truly believed in her vision and were counting on her to make them their next million.

No pressure.

Everyone had careers, and Jill was well on her way, to either a major success or a major disaster. Her scientist parents and big brother, Ryan, thought she was nuts. And, she had to admit, Wildfire Ridge had been a huge undertaking with a chance at an equally spectacular fail. But with her organizational skills and inability to take shit from anybody, Jill was one month away from making her dream come true.

She just hoped there would be no complications with Chris, er, Sam.

When he'd flashed her that easy grin, she had to admit she thought about their one night together. A lot. She was thinking about it so much it was hard to let another thought into her head. And if she couldn't talk about this to her two best friends in the world, who could she talk to?

"Remember the Chris sighting three years ago in San Francisco?" Jill said.

"How could I forget?" Carly took a sugar packet away from Grace. "You talked about it for weeks."

"That was the last Chris sighting until Levi came around," Zoey said.

On one particularly long and boring afternoon at The Drip when they all still worked together, after their three o'clock dance off, Jill had devised a complicated scale for rating men. It was called the Chris Scale because the mean was based on all the well-known Chrises: Pratt, Evans, Pine, Hemsworth. For a man to rate high on the scale meant he'd passed the mean. This was a big deal, naturally, as the mean was already high. Not that she thought all men had to offer were their looks, far from it. But the Chris Scale was, to this date, the only way she liked doing math.

"I have a confession to make." Jill moved the sugar packets away from Grace. Her reach was getting long.

"Oh, this should be interesting," Carly said.

"I may have done more than simply rate this 'Chris.' I may have spent some time with him."

"How much time?" Zoey narrowed her eyes.

Jill inspected her fingernails. She needed a good manicure. "Um, all night?"

Zoey slapped the table. "Dude! You said you'd never done that before. A one-night stand?"

"Well, it was just this *once*. I figured… I needed it. Deserved it."

"Right on." Carly laughed.

"Look, I'm the one who's been celibate for three years. That night has had to last me a long time. Three years!"

"It's been even longer for me," Zoey protested. "I'm not even going to say how long."

"Aw," Jill said, hugging Zoey.

Jill and Zoey both turned to Carly.

"This morning, before Grace woke up."

"You're not even supposed to be *able* to have morning sex when you have a baby!" Jill said.

"I know, right?" Carly kissed Grace's plump cheek. "She's possibly the best baby ever."

Zoey glanced lovingly to Grace, then outside to Boo. "I don't see why you can bring her in here and I can't bring Boo in. He'd behave."

Carly wrinkled her nose, but apparently chose to ignore the comparison of her stepdaughter to a well-trained Great Dane.

"So what are the men like who showed up today?" Carly said. "Anyone to help you, um, get over that dry spell?"

"Funny you should mention that," Jill said. "Because Chris? He's one of my guys. Except his name is Sam."

"Get out! Chris is *here*?" Carly squealed.

"His name is Sam."

"Sam, Chris, what's the difference if he's hot?" Zoey said.

"You forget," Jill said with great patience. "I'm now his boss. As in, he's my employee. As in lawsuit waiting to happen."

Carly snorted. "Technically, Levi was my boss for a while when I was Grace's nanny."

"But you and Levi fell in love. Maybe I don't want to get sued."

Both of her friends looked at her expectantly. She'd never been one to doubt equality, both in the workplace and the bedroom. But now... Well, it was a little icky to come on to her employee. And there was the whole ethical/legal dilemma. She couldn't ignore that issue even if she wanted to. If her investors were to find out they might think her less than professional.

Besides, she'd be twenty-eight this year. Even if she'd never had a one-night stand before Sam, she had a past filled with go-nowhere relationships with Class A commitment-phobes. And for the first time, she wondered what that said about her. Why did she always wind up with men who were in some fashion or another unavailable? While her mother might have something to say about that, Jill was sure she didn't want to hear it. Point being, she had to learn to want a man who was available to her, and that certainly wasn't her employee.

And that night in San Francisco, it hadn't been Jill in Sam's arms. It had been her alter ego, Angelina. That Angelina was a wild woman. She was fearless.

"It was one night." One wild and crazy night she allowed herself. A little fun for once with no strings. "He wasn't supposed to be a part of my daily life."

"Well, now he is," Carly said.

"Thanks for the 411," Jill deadpanned.

"Oh my God, you're not going to fire him, are you?" Zoey looked on the verge of tears. "He might need this job."

Jill patted bleeding-heart Zoey's hands. "No, of course not. I'll just make it work. Take a hands-off approach. Lay down the law and all that."

"You're so good at that," Zoey said.

"But wait," Carly said. "Maybe there's something you're not telling us."

"Right." Zoey turned to Carly. "Like…what?"

"Like he wasn't any good." Carly set Grace back in her stroller and handed her a set of plastic keys. "Looks aren't everything. Maybe he was high on the Chris Scale, but um, you know, was 'lacking' in other vital ways."

That would have been nice. Or rather convenient. Not then, but now.

"No." She cleared her throat. "Not lacking. At all. In any way."

Carly grinned. "I see."

Wrong though it seemed for someone she'd met once, Sam had been the best she'd ever had. And if it was going to be difficult to work with him, day in, day out, watching him all sweaty, challenging himself physically, working hard… Well, she was up to the task. She would look but not touch. A woman had to get her kicks somewhere.

Hers was a tough job, but hey, someone had to do it.

Chapter Three

Later that evening, Jill went back to the office trailer as she often did, this time to work on the bookkeeping she'd been avoiding. She had stacks of receipts to enter into a spreadsheet so the accountant could put together the next financial report for their board of investors. The board already wanted her to hire a general manager to report directly to them. They really needed a receptionist and scheduler since lately the phone had been ringing off the hook for bookings. Now that they were a month away from opening, all their advertising was coming to fruition and they were booked six months in advance for the most popular events. The bookings could be outsourced but Jill did this herself, too.

The office phone rang, and heck, since she was here at nine o'clock, she picked it up. "Wildfire Ridge Outdoor Adventures. How can I help you?"

"Hi! I thought I was going to be talking to a machine.

We're having a big family reunion and want to water-ski and kayak. You guys do that?" a woman's voice said.

"Absolutely. Our Anderson Lake here on the ridge is equipped for all that. Where did you hear about us?"

"Your Facebook page and one of my friends."

Good to know all her hard work for the business was working. She should probably spend more time on social media. She spent several more minutes talking with the woman, who was arranging a fortieth anniversary surprise for her parents.

Guess it was high time to hire some more administrative help. For her, the guides had come first, and she'd wanted to pay them a decent salary so she'd insisted that most of their initial payroll budget go to that.

But Jill seriously should spread the workload around so she could focus on her strengths—marketing and growing the business. She wanted to hire a general manager, but she'd looked through stacks of résumés and they all seemed like corporate drones to her. She wanted someone else who would put their heart into this business the way she had. Anyway, she didn't even have the time to interview anyone. She'd simply taken on all the work herself and made the job her life for the last year.

Jill understood hard work. She had studied business at Cal Poly, trying to find her place in the world of high finance. Aiming high, after all, was the Davis way. With her father the doctor and mother the scientist setting the bar, it was always just high enough to be out of Jill's reach. Then her older brother, Ryan, her hero since the time she was a child, had made his own way. Shown Jill there was another way to succeed. He'd gone to West Point, become an officer and later a decorated war hero. Now he was the newly elected youngest Sheriff in Fortune.

No one in her family did anything halfway.

No one other than Jill. She'd dropped out of business school when she realized she'd never be happy in corporate America. Not what her parents pictured for their straight-A-earning daughter, but they'd never understood her anyway. Never accepted that she didn't quite fit in with the Davis family.

She'd always had an entrepreneurial spirit instead of an academic spirit, and loved a well-placed challenge. She'd been scouting locations to open a B and B in Fortune when she'd happened upon an article in the local newspaper about the employment challenges for young veterans coming back from the war. The next thing she knew she'd worked out a business plan for an outdoor adventure company, hiring veterans to be the guides.

The park would open in a month's time. She needed the men to help finalize the courses and do test excursions for their first group of booked test clients.

An hour later, Jill rubbed the heel of her bare foot, leaned away from the monitor and stretched her aching back. For someone who would launch an outdoor adventure company, she was spending far too much time on her behind lately. She managed to hit the gym for her scheduled torture twice a week, but being around all these hard bodies, that wasn't going to be enough.

She stood up, stretched again and forced herself to do fifty jumping jacks. Out of breath and sweating, she took a break and went to her window. The side of her trailer faced Sam's, but that's not why she'd assigned it to him. It only made sense that since he'd been enthusiastic enough to arrive early, he deserved the bigger trailer. There was no other reason.

She peeked through her window's blinds. And there, framed by a sliver of moonlight, she caught the distinct figure of Sam's back, hunched over the fire pit. He was with the other guys that had come in after him. Michael, Ty and Julian. They were laughing and seemed to be enjoying themselves.

Sam poked at the fire. He looked over his shoulder in her direction. And caught her staring.

"Oh crap."

She quickly shut the window blinds to give the men their privacy. The last thing they'd want is a boss who lived here 24-7 spying on them. They could take care of themselves and didn't need *her* guidance. She trusted them, too, and wanted them to know it. And she also didn't want Sam to think she was lusting after him, because the man already had enough confidence in himself.

For good reason.

She headed back to her desk to shut down her laptop. Rather than get the attention of the men as she left her trailer, maybe she'd sleep on the little cot she kept in here. Sleeping here was a good way to annoy Ryan, who hated the thought of her up here on the hill at nights by herself. He'd made her promise not to do it again after catching her a month ago. And she hadn't since, but tonight was different. Tonight she wasn't alone on the hill with the occasional mountain lion and deer.

There was a rapping on her trailer door. Jill's head jerked up, she stood, and in her haste, she tripped over her shoes and nearly landed on the floor. Instead of falling, she braced against one thin aluminum wall, which jostled with the weight of her body. *Great.* Stuck up on a flagpole and almost falling on her butt. She was such a prize.

"Jill." Sam's voice.

"I'll be right with you!" She quickly stood and toed one flat back on, then the other.

"You okay in there?"

"Fine."

"You don't sound fine."

"Well, I am!"

"This doesn't have to be an argument."

She opened the door and shoved on a smile. "Can I help you?"

"No," he said, stepping inside. "But maybe I can help you."

"That's not necessary. I just tripped over my…shoes. There isn't much room in here, you know." *A little defensive, are we, Jill?*

"That's not what I meant." He glanced around the room. "But you're right. Since it looks like you're trying to sleep here, too."

Sam was dressed as he had been earlier, but now his square jaw was darkened with stubble. It was the scruffy, just-rolled-out-of-bed look that drove most women crazy. She was no exception.

"I don't do that anymore. Much. My brother wasn't too crazy about me sleeping out here alone."

He quirked a brow. "I'm not too crazy about it, either."

"I can assure you I'm not going to go next door to your trailer and attack you once the sun goes down."

Again. A little sensitive, are we?

He gave her a slow smile. "I was actually thinking that my cot is much bigger than your cot."

She was a little taken aback, not that she should be. "You're not shy, are you?"

"You should know that about me."

Funny, she did. But what he didn't remember, apparently, or maybe had just chosen to ignore, was that she'd come on to *him*. He'd been sitting alone in the bar, nursing his beer for most of the night, looking like someone who'd lost his best friend. He hadn't talked or had a smile for anyone, not even the leering cocktail waitress who kept "accidentally" brushing her breasts against him. He might as well have been wearing a sign that read: Do Not Approach—Dangerous When Provoked. Besides nursing a beer and giving surly looks to anyone who approached, he rolled a coin between the fingers of his right hand over and over again.

And yes, she'd been intrigued.

Nothing had changed in that regard, she had to admit, but now he knew she was a natural redhead. She knew what his sex voice sounded like. And he knew hers.

Sue her if she thought that two people who'd been horizontal should know a lot more about each other. But even so, were she still into rating her mistakes, of which there were many, he'd be, hands down, her favorite one.

"W-why did you knock? Do you need something?"

"Wanted to tell you that you've hired a first-rate group of men out there." He nudged his chin. "All of them former Army, but I don't hold that against them."

"Thank you. That's…great."

"And we're on board with what you're trying to do here."

"That means a lot to me."

His gaze did a slow slide up her body and she became intensely aware of the heat of the day.

"Was there anyone special to you in the service?"

"My big brother. Ryan. He went to West Point."

See, this was the kind of get-to-know-you conversation she should have had with him *before* going to bed with him. He hadn't been all that much into talking that night and frankly, at that time she hadn't needed conversation.

Sam quirked a brow. "An officer. I won't hold that against him, either."

"Actually, he was infantry and got hurt. They gave him a medal."

Why was her voice so shaky? That was a while back and she was over it now. Besides, Ryan hated any talk about "the medal."

"Sorry. Most of the officers I knew didn't get their hands dirty."

"That's not Ryan." Her chin rose. "And please forget about the medal. He hates when I talk about it, or tell anyone."

"Got it."

She leaned on her desk, arms folded across her chest. "You know, I was just thinking that we know very little about each other."

"That's true. I didn't even know you *had* a brother."

She pointed. "Exactly. Now you know something about me you didn't before. I should know something about you."

He narrowed his eyes. "Such as…?"

"Anything. Just one thing about you that I don't know."
Why don't you have an emergency contact?

"I like dogs. Grew up with Labs and missed having one while I was away. I intend to adopt one first chance I get."

"Good to know." That certainly hadn't come up the night they'd spent together, but it also wasn't quite what she meant and he knew it. "And why don't you have an emergency contact?"

He frowned. "You said one thing."

"Okay. One thing a day."

"You're pushing it."

"But you owe me." She took a breath. "For the most incredible night of your life. For rocking your world."

Hell, yeah. No one ever said she lacked confidence, either. Or, at least, was extremely good at faking it.

He gave her another slow smile, with a panty-melting heat in his gaze. "Point taken."

Suddenly it was a little too hot in here, like August had landed only in the perimeter of this trailer and the approximate two feet of distance between them. She tried not to look at him. "You should probably go now, before the guys start to wonder."

"Whether I'm in here being ravaged by the boss?"

"Or something."

He opened his mouth to speak, and she could almost see the wheels spinning in his brain, but then he turned to go.

She suddenly had a fleeting and terrible thought. "You didn't tell them about us, did you?"

He scowled, and she flashed back to that night and the same irritated look he'd had on his face until she'd given him something else to think about.

"Hell, no. That's between you and me. Always will be."

He smiled again, and then he was gone.

Chapter Four

When Sam woke before dawn the next morning, he did not immediately recognize his surroundings. He froze, his heart rate must have hit the triple digits, and sweat poured off him.

Tim and Dave were dead. They were gone.

"The threat's been neutralized."

No. That happened a while ago. It wasn't happening now. He shook the memory off, tossing and turning, eventually kicking off the soft cotton sheets.

Man, how he hated this. Hated the fear that shot through him as he fought to slow his heart rate down. Fought to forget. Fought to remember. He was home. Safe. He was back in the Bay Area. Fortune, to be exact. In a trailer on Wildfire Ridge.

And just like that his thoughts turned to his Angelina. Angelina, who was *not* Angelina. She was Jill, and still every bit as gorgeous as he remembered. Since he'd thought back to that single night many times over the past three years, he'd recognized her the minute he heard her voice. Heard the sound of her nervous laughter. Saw her long red hair whipping in the wind. Her equally long legs curved around that flagpole. Told himself he had to be imagining things. A look-alike, maybe. He'd waited until she was inches away from him to be sure he wasn't hallucinating.

The night they'd met, he'd been in San Francisco on leave. He should have dropped in on his parents, who were not that far away. Not a long drive to the other side of the bay and Berkeley. He could have called them, let them know he was stateside, and he'd struggled that night to make the right choice. In the end, he couldn't do it. In the end, a tall redhead had made her way to his table and made him an offer he couldn't refuse.

And good thing, too, because he didn't think he would have made it through the next three years without the memory of her. Of that night. The knowledge that it was possible to get so lost in someone you forgot everything else. It was possible to forget the fear and the guilt and the pain. Possible to simply allow himself to feel *something good* again because she made it difficult not to do just that. He hadn't wanted to hold back from her that night, but he had. Everything but the physical. And so had she. She'd been the one to suggest the fake names.

Just one perfect night.

Without the pressure of knowing he'd eventually drive her away like he had everyone else, he handled that one night. One day at a time was the only way he could manage his life.

Everything was different now. She was here, and she was his boss. A man did not mess with that.

He hadn't expected the form to be a problem, but something told him she wouldn't leave this alone. She wanted to know why he wasn't in touch with his parents. Why he didn't think enough of their relationship to put their names on a form.

Hell, it took a lot for him to put someone's name on a damn form.

Right now, he wasn't interested in talking to them, and he didn't see that changing anytime soon. So no, their names weren't going on her damn form.

He dressed quickly and went for a run, the cool spring morning air waking him so he was no longer groggy from lack of sleep. Then he hit the shower, and thought about coffee. Sure enough, his employer had been more than generous and stocked the kitchen with some essentials. He had his coffee and was out the door by 6:00 a.m. One by one, the men came out of their separate trailers on the grounds until all of them were gathered outside the office trailer.

No Jill anywhere in sight.

"What do you think 'bright and early' means to her?" Michael said.

"She didn't give us a time," Ty said with a shrug.

"Strikes me as being new to this boss thing," Julian said.

It had struck Sam the same. Granted, he'd never asked about her occupation nor had any interest in knowing. In his fantasies, she'd had many jobs and not one of them had been owner and manager of an outdoor adventure company. *Stripper?* Yes. *Masseuse?* Hell, yes. *Naughty nurse?* Possibly. *Porn star?* Definitely.

"She'll be here."

And an hour later, as the guys stood around debating whether the Warriors would take the championship again this year, she drove up the hill. She parked her sedan a few feet away from the office trailer. When she noticed them all standing there, she did a double take, then seemed to mutter something to herself as she opened the driver's side door.

"Hot damn, she's cute," Julian said.

"Yeah."

Sam had been thinking the same thing. Thinking how she made him want to smile. Made him want to do a lot of other things, too, first and foremost making her smile. And scream out his name again. This time his real one.

"Usually I don't even like redheads. Too bad she's the boss," Julian said.

"Exactly," Sam said firmly.

There was some relief in realizing that he wasn't the only one who couldn't have her.

Jill walked down the path to the office trailer, carrying several plastic shopping bags in her arms. Her hair was up in a ponytail today; she wore long hiking pants and a tight-fitting black performance tee that read, Wildfire Ridge's Outdoor Adventures in red stitching across her right breast. Hiking boots, too.

"Good morning." She set the plastic bags on the benched picnic table near the trailer. "Everyone grab a shirt. Mostly large and extra-large, and they run small."

Sam grabbed one first. He pulled off his shirt and tugged the other one on and the others followed suit. If Jill seemed shocked that they'd take their shirts off in front of her, she didn't say anything.

She went into a welcome speech that, while it sounded sincere, also might have been scripted. She looked nervous to Sam, not that he should know. He'd never seen nervous Jill before.

Next was a discussion about equipment sorting.

"We had a delivery two days ago, and I need help inventorying. Next I'd like each of you to try out all the courses and give me your feedback. Is it challenging enough for you guides, and if so, is there a way to level it so that we can work with, um…"

"Different levels of fitness?" Sam offered.

She snapped her fingers. "Yes, exactly. And we've got our first group of testers coming out next week so we want to be ready."

"We got you covered, boss." Julian winked.

"Thanks! Oh, and another thing. I'll eventually want to take photos of you guides doing some of the activities so I can put them on our Facebook page."

The next few hours were like family camp on steroids. Leadership came naturally to him, so he wound up organizing the guys as they pulled equipment out of boxes, counted and categorized. The fun part was trying out some of the equipment. The zip line stretched across a small canyon that was nevertheless about 100 feet up and a long drop. It was obvious some great engineering had gone into it. After each of them had gone across the zip line twice, Sam decided they were having too much fun to be technically working. At least, he was.

"Next," he found himself ordering.

Julian, Ty and Michael went ahead to the rock face that looked to have been partially man-made, working with some of the rockier and craggier areas of the hilltop. He was about to follow when he saw Jill staring at the zip line from a few feet away.

"Want a go at this?"

She shook her head a little violently. "Oh no. I've got paperwork to get back to. I just wanted to check on you guys. I see everything's going smoothly."

"Well…"

"Oh God. What's wrong? Tell me."

"You can dial back on the panic mode. The comm system has some bugs in it. You might want to look into that."

"Not again. I've called twice and every time they fix it, it goes down again. Is that it?"

"And I was just going to suggest you have a rescue plan in place."

She chewed on her lower lip. "Working on one. For the Sheriff. He wants me to get it to him soon."

"How soon?"

"Tomorrow morning?"

He winced. "Okay, I can help. Let me look over what you have. It should be fairly simple."

"Or I could ask Ryan for an extension. Again." She blew out a breath. "I can tell you right now he won't like it."

"Your brother, Ryan? *He's* the Sheriff?"

"I'm sorry, did I not mention that?"

"You didn't. What does he think about all this?" He waved to the expanse of the hilltop and the land around them. There had to be a good two hundred acres or more here. A large man-made lake with a dock and an array of boats and kayaks. The land was mostly undeveloped other than the park and he had to wonder how difficult it must have been to get both the funding and the approval on a project this size.

"He's supportive." She folded her arms across her generous rack, which he had to admit was further emphasized by the rather snug fit of that shirt. He was beginning to love their new company tees. "Okay, see. That's one more thing you now know about me. Your turn."

He didn't like this. It was a clear manipulation and he'd never been into these types of games with women. She was prying, and he knew it. He also realized she wouldn't give up. Someone who'd taken on a challenge of this magnitude didn't give up easily.

Using his equally strong manipulation skills, he ignored her. "We should talk about what you have for a plan so far. Let me see what you've got."

"You'd do that?"

"I would."

"This isn't just your attempt to make us more than a one-hit wonder?" She held up finger quotes.

"Nah. I'm all business right now."

She grinned, but he wasn't sure it was certainty he saw in her green eyes or concern. "Drop by after you guys knock off. I'm sure I'll still be in the office."

She apparently spent too much time at work. Probably not healthy, but at the moment it would benefit him.

After the workday ended, the guys were headed down the hill and toward town and a bar called the Silver Saddle. He begged off joining them, as he was always more clearheaded without a drink. Instead, he hit the shower and changed. The light was still on in the office trailer, so he knocked once and let himself in. And found Jill doing jumping jacks.

This was not helpful to his all-business approach. She had her back to the door, turning slowly in a circle, and apparently hadn't heard him come in. The earbuds, probably. But the way she was going, she'd turn in his direction any second now.

"It's raining men!" she sang out.

He smiled as she bounced in the direction of the door and tried hard to appear... Wet.

"It's...oh." She stopped and pulled earbuds out. "Sorry."

"Nothing to be sorry about." He bit back a chuckle.

"It's just that I've been working so hard lately to get everything ready for grand opening that I never get to the gym anymore. Every hour or so I try to remember to take a break and do some jumping jacks."

"Get the blood pumping."

"That's right." Breathing hard, she walked back to her desk.

"On the other hand, there's a lot you could do right outside the trailer door." He pointed.

"Yes, and I'll get to it. This is just easier right now. Convenient. But I can't wait to try the zip line."

"Looks like some good engineering went into it."

"It cost us enough." She opened up her laptop and pushed papers aside. "I've got the search and rescue plan in here. I had some help from a couple of firefighters from the rescue squad and I did some research of my own. I'll just print it out for you."

"No need. I'll read from here." He sidled up behind her, kneeling to see just over her shoulder. And smell her hair. Coconut.

She shot up suddenly. "Here, you sit."

He took her seat, gratified he made her nervous. "You just continue with your jacks. Give me fifty."

"Uh, no thanks. I'm okay for the next hour." She stood behind him, looking over his shoulder. "And don't think I forgot you haven't told me your one thing yet."

"Oh yeah. That."

"You thought you distracted me, but you now know two things about me that you didn't before. I have a brother who was in the service *and* he's the Sheriff. I know you like dogs, which, BTW, is not big news. Everyone likes dogs! Now it's your turn."

"True enough," he said, perusing her plan. "I like cats, too, and that one isn't as common."

She let out an exasperated sigh, which sounded like a cross between a groan and a moan. Again, not helpful to this all-business attitude he was trying to keep with her.

"That doesn't count! Look, I know you're from the Bay Area. It's the one thing I knew about you that night."

"Yeah?" He didn't like where this was headed. If she didn't stop pushing, maybe this job wouldn't work out.

"Is your family in the Bay Area?"

He turned to look up at her. "I don't talk to my parents anymore. It would be stupid as hell to put them on your damn form. And that's your one thing. It's big enough that it should take me through tomorrow, too."

Shockingly, she seemed to agree, nodding quietly.

"Do you trust me?" he asked now. "Because you should."

"You know I do. I realize you could have taken advantage of me that night, but you didn't."

"No more than you took advantage of me."

"Yes, but you know. You're a guy."

"I'm aware of that, thanks."

"Anyway, I feel like we both took advantage of the *situation*."

"Equal opportunity advantage."

"Right."

An hour later, thank God, she'd quieted down and sat on the edge of the cot, reading from her Kindle. She looked up at him. "Are you almost done?"

"Almost. Just needed to dot some *i*'s."

Liar. He'd pretty much revamped the entire plan to be much more in line with serious search and rescue. What she'd had was serviceable but did not account for all possibilities. Might as well plan for everything.

A few more minutes later, he stretched and leaned back in the chair, satisfied. "Okay. Done."

No answer. She was asleep on the cot, clutching her Kindle.

Just the sight of her lying there, a lock of her hair covering one of her eyes, caused a strong pull of lust to flicker through him. He should get out of here. Nights in particular he didn't feel human, and watching her sleep wasn't helping. This felt like a moment when he should *do* something. Something helpful. What did a civilian do in a situation like this? He needed to remember how to be *normal* again. Should he wake her up so she could drive home? Let her sleep? Pretty sure he shouldn't touch her. He didn't have the right.

He took the Kindle from her death grip and set it on the desk. Drew the covers up to her neck, managing not to touch her. She didn't move but continued to sleep like a rock. Her face, normally so animated and open, was now relaxed and strangely vulnerable.

And he couldn't stop looking at her.

He'd never watched her sleep and felt a little voyeuristic doing that now. Like he had intruded on her private personal space. Not that she wasn't trying hard to intrude into *his* private world. But she wasn't going to get an all-access pass into his personal life. He couldn't allow that. She was his boss now and nothing more. He shouldn't want anything more.

"One-hit wonder."

She could be right about that. Sure would make his job here easier. He couldn't take care of anyone else when he could barely take care of himself. He hadn't managed to get rid of the nightmares, had he? Waking up in a cold sweat had become the norm. And while the memory of her had been enough to get him through some rough nights in the past, her proximity now wasn't doing the same. Instead of comforting him, she was making him itchy and wary of what he wanted. What he didn't deserve and shouldn't have.

Making sure her trailer door was locked and secure, he made his way next door to his trailer. Alone.

Chapter Five

"This coffee tastes like death! You know how picky I am about my coffee. Can't you do any better than this?" Jill pushed the foam cup of black sludge across Ryan's desk.

He had been hunched over her search and rescue plan for the past few minutes, reading. "Shh, woman. You don't want to anger her."

She followed his gaze to his deputy admin, Renata Dooley, a woman one did not mess with. She was German, and at six feet tall the largest woman Jill had ever known. She took shit from no one and she'd worked for the Sheriff's office for approximately forever.

"She makes the coffee?" Jill whispered. "It's horrible."

"Yeah, well, that's not her job." Ryan tapped the paper in front of him. "Did you put this plan together?"

"Yes, um, why?"

"It's just so...detailed. You thought of everything."

"I had a little help."

Sam, frankly, had kicked ass on this plan. This morning when she'd woken on the office cot yet again, drool dried on her cheek, she had a blanket covering her that she didn't remember putting there. Her Kindle not on the floor where it usually landed, but placed carefully on her desk. And the plan on her desk, complete and perfect.

"Yeah?"

"One of my guys is a former Marine. He's very detail-oriented."

Ryan didn't know the half of it.

"A Marine?" He winced. "Christ, Jill. All of these men were checked out by the agency, right? References, backgrounds, everything?"

"Yes, *Ryan*." She'd been over this with him before.

Her big brother had always been over-the-top protective. Not entirely his fault. Their parents had put in long hours on the job and even if he was only four years older, Ryan had practically raised her.

He set the papers down. "This is good. I'm satisfied. I'm sure the city council will be, too."

"What do they have to do with it?"

"They want me to bring it to the next meeting."

She knew well that Ryan hated the politics of being Sheriff, but he'd accepted the nomination because he cared about the town of Fortune.

"Boy, they just can't stay out of my business, can they?"

"You should have expected this. Small-town growth restrictions," Ryan said.

"But this is going to be so special for our town. No one in the Bay Area has anything like this park."

"Exactly. It's going to bring a lot of traffic our way. And you know how the city council feels about traffic."

Holy wow, did she know. She regularly got an earful.

"It's also going to bring in sales tax dollars. And anyway, they don't seem to mind the traffic when it's a new housing development."

"You'll get no argument from me. I personally can't wait to try out the zip line or go wakeboarding. First, I need some time off."

"Speaking of time off, do you know if Mom or Dad are going to make the grand opening?"

"They haven't told you?"

"No."

Ryan rubbed his forehead. "Dad's speaking at a medical conference next month. The opportunity came up and he and Mom are going to make a trip of it. Paris."

"Oh."

"I can't believe they didn't tell you yet."

"Well, it's Paris. I probably wouldn't come to my grand opening, either. No big deal." She stood.

"It *is* a big deal."

"Not really. It's not like I've written an academic paper." *Or won the Medal of Honor.*

"You know I'll be there. I wouldn't miss it."

She grinned. "And you'll bring a date?"

"Stop busting my chops. You know I have no time to date."

"Make time."

"Look who's talking. You haven't had a date in what? Three years?"

Don't remind me. "Yes, but I'm not the one depriving some child-to-be of your dimples."

"For the love of God, not you, too. It's enough that Mom's on my case about settling down."

"Speaking as your little sister, who wants to be an aunt someday, I just want you to be happy."

"And speaking as your big brother, who doesn't mind waiting to be an uncle, I just want you to be safe."

"Oh, I will be."

She bussed her brother's cheek and was out the door.

Back in the safety and quiet of her sedan, Jill took her cell phone out and dialed her mother. Always best to get the unpleasantness out of the way fast. Unlike Mom, Jill had learned the hard way that there was no point in avoiding their difficult relationship.

"Hi, honey," Mom answered on the third ring. "I've been meaning to—"

"I just heard you can't attend the grand opening because of Paris."

"Your father was invited to lecture at a medical conference."

"Mom, I told you guys about this months ago."

"I know, and I'm so sorry to miss your…your…"

"Grand opening."

Jill sighed. She was used to it by now. Mom, a brilliant woman, had some kind of hiccup in her brain synapses when it came to Jill's so-called "hobbies."

"I really am so sorry to miss it. It sounds like such fun."

Fun. Not hard work that kept her in the office so late she'd actually taken to sleeping there. "Yeah, fun, but also we're *doing something* here. Building something. Providing work to veterans and creating a business that's going to benefit the entire town, too."

"You have such a big heart."

Now Mom made it sound like charity, which it wasn't. Not in a million years would she take pity on veterans. She needed them and they needed her.

"Okay. Have fun in Paris. And tell Dad congrats on the invitation."

She hung up and tossed the phone on the passenger seat. When her parents had first heard about her plans, they'd freaked.

"Extreme sports? Are you out of your mind?"

No amount of assurance from her that *she* wasn't going to be the one participating in the more dangerous extreme sports seemed to help. She wanted to. Little interested her more than an athlete's ability to push beyond their physical boundaries. To move past what one would expect the human body capable of. She enjoyed cycling and hikes, though she'd been too busy to get outdoors for some time. An irony she did not miss. Feet away from some great outdoor activities and with no time for them.

When she got back to the ridge, she noticed the guys off in the distance, stacking the rock climbing equipment. Ropes and pulleys. Sam always seemed to be in charge, even if they were all technically on the same level. She knew from their personnel records that at thirty he was only slightly older than the other men. But according to the agency, Sam was leadership material and should be treated as such.

She walked closer to the men, enjoying the view. Big brawny men hard at work. It wasn't true, as Zoey and Carly often teased, that she'd started this business so she could hang out with good-looking and physically active men. Just a perk. She whipped out her phone camera and took a few photos of the men before they'd noticed her. But it wasn't long before they did notice, and Julian was the first to preen and pose for the camera.

"Get my good side," he said turning to his left and squeezing a bicep.

"You don't have one," Sam said.

"Seriously, guys. I want some good photos of you to

put on the Facebook page. This is better if you go about your business and ignore me."

That worked for a few minutes and she got some great shots of Sam climbing the rock with Julian belaying him. She zoomed in for a shot of Sam as he turned and smiled at nothing in particular as he neared the top of the rock. God, he was gorgeous. She studied the photo of him smiling, the sun glinting off his golden-brown hair.

In the end, she had to force herself to quit all the drooling and get back to some of her chores. First, she took an invigorating walk along the property, reminding herself of all she'd done here. Much as she would have appreciated her parents being at the grand opening, this at least insured that should something fail, they wouldn't have to see her fall flat on her face.

But they were *not* going to fail here. Yes, that's right. Fake it till you make it, Jill Davis. Believe it. Kick ass. Every day is a new day to win. She had that particular affirmation stuck to her laptop so she'd see it every morning.

A few minutes later, she somehow found herself at the zip line again, staring into the canyon below. She sucked in a breath and took a step back. Then another.

It wasn't heights she was technically afraid of, but the falling part tripped her up every time. This zip line had been made by some of the best engineers in the valley with top-notch equipment. But try telling that to her parents. They'd just ask her whether she thought it was wise to take such chances with her health. Even though she'd been healthy now for *years*.

Definitely, without a doubt, she was going to go across the canyon on that zip line. She couldn't wait.

"You know you want it. You want it bad."

Sam's voice, from just behind her. Deep and sexy.

Their chemistry and connection made the air snap and crackle between them. It was addictive. She turned to remind him that, despite what she felt, they were never—not very probably, anyway—going to happen again.

He was looking past her, nodding in the direction of the zip line. Oh yeah. That.

She wanted that, too.

"I do. I just haven't had the time."

"Uh-huh." He didn't seem convinced, oddly enough. "I'll take you. Nothing to be afraid of."

"Did I say I was afraid?" She went hand on hip.

He shook his head as though deciding it wasn't worth arguing about. "Someone needs to go to the hardware store."

"What do we need?"

"Rope. There are some rocky areas we should cordon off for safety reasons."

"Right. Okay, I'll go." She headed back to her trailer to get the keys.

When she returned, Sam sat in the front driver's side seat of her sedan.

"Hey," she said, opening the already unlocked door. "What are you doing?"

He held out his hand. "Driving."

"No, you're not."

"Hand me the keys. I drive faster than you do."

"How do you figure?"

He quirked a brow. "I drive faster than most people. No offense."

Aha! One more thing she knew about him, and she hadn't pried it out of him. He drove fast. Probably had a bunch of speeding tickets. Reluctantly, but figuring she was ahead of the game, she handed him her keys.

"I *can* get the rope for you."

"Didn't want you to come back with the wrong kind."

She made her way to the passenger seat, fuming a little bit but not wanting to argue with him, and shut the door. "How many different types of ropes can there be?"

"The things I could teach you." He started up the car.

So he was this kind of guy. The kind that thought he could make the best decisions on everything from what he should have for dinner to what she should have for dinner. She wouldn't have guessed this about him. Good. This was a huge turnoff. She needed him to behave like this and before long she'd hate him so much there would no longer be any romantic tension between them.

"Okay, *you* drive. *You* pick the rope."

He peeled down the hill and she grabbed hold of the handle bar. She couldn't remember the last time she'd done that. Sam must be an adrenaline junkie about everything. She could be an adrenaline junkie, too, if she wanted to be.

"Did I *mention* my brother is the Sheriff?"

He didn't say a word but gave her a sideways glance as they rolled down the hill. The minute they pulled out onto the highway, he slowed some, riding the speed limit to the edge but never going over it. He drove them through town in the right direction, apparently already knowing the location of the only hardware store in town, Mack's.

Jill broke the silence. "About this speed issue."

"Who said it's an issue?"

Oh brother. "Got many speeding tickets?"

"Define 'many.' I had a few." He rolled down the window. "Just realized I gave you something else you didn't know about me."

Damn! He didn't miss much, did he? "I could have guessed that about you."

"But you didn't." He gazed at her from underneath his eyelashes. "I need something from you now."

She let out a breath and considered how honest she could be. "I didn't drive until I was eighteen."

"Yeah?" He seemed genuinely curious. "Why?"

Should she tell him her parents were so overprotective they wouldn't allow her to get her license until then? They'd done a statistical analysis and found that fatal accidents dropped at age seventeen and then significantly at age eighteen.

And while she'd excelled at knocking down every one of their objections and worries, she couldn't argue with their stupid statistics in black and white. They hadn't budged on this issue no matter how hard she'd tried.

"That was one thing." Two could play this game.

He scowled, appearing slightly irritated that she wasn't going to run her mouth off. "Fair enough."

A few minutes later, he'd parked and led her to the rope section of the store. And holy cannoli, he was right. She stared in shock at the display. There were as many types of ropes as there were types of bras. With bras, you had your strapless, underwire, lace, satin, demi cup and push-up—her favorite.

When it came to rope, it appeared there was nylon, polypropylene, manila, parachute, Kevlar, bungee shock, three-strand combo, combo...

"When did this all get so complicated?" She was beginning to think maybe he hadn't considered her a total idiot for doubting she could pick the right kind of rope.

"Different ropes for different jobs," he said as he grabbed several of a certain type. "For instance, if you're going to tie someone up you need one kind of rope, if you—"

"Excuse me?"

"You need the right type."

"No, back up to the part where you tie someone up."

He simply stared at her.

"Okay, never...never mind."

"That's probably best." He grinned.

Oh boy.

After she'd paid for the purchase of three different kinds of rope with her business card, Sam offered her the keys. "Sorry. I get a little pushy sometimes."

"That's okay," she said reflexively even though it hadn't been. "At least you apologized."

"You're not used to apologies?"

"Let's say it's not the norm." She started up the car. "I dated men who weren't into apologizing. Because mainly, according to them, they were never wrong."

He snorted. "Sounds like you dated the wrong kind of men."

She was close to asking him if there *was* a right kind of man, but decided it was a subject best not approached by a boss with her employee and one-night stand. She'd started to redefine her perfect man recently, and while Sam had the looks going for him, and he excelled at the physical part, he didn't have much else on her list. Sure, it was an evolving list and as Carly continually reminded her, she'd likely never get everything on it.

"Gotta ask you," Sam said. "The guys and I were all wondering. Why an extreme adventures park?"

"Well, it was either that or a B and B."

While that wasn't exactly true, it was the simplest answer to give him. The real answer was far more complicated. It partly involved her desire to help veterans find work and feel needed again, and Sam might take that the wrong way. She drove toward the ridge, taking it much slower than Sam had to make a point. Or maybe to spend a little more time with him and possibly get in another nugget about him. Either way.

"Those two things are nothing alike."

"Yes, thanks for noticing. I'd have had a much easier time with a B and B."

"Again. Why?"

"Have you ever watched the Olympics?"

"Yep. Downhill skiing."

"For me it was the ice-skating. The amazing control. Not just all the balance and strength but incredible grace. I'm in awe of someone who has mastered control over their physical body to that extent." She glanced at him. "In some small way, I wanted to be a part of that. Challenging the body to much more than you ever believed possible."

He seemed satisfied with that answer because he nodded.

"And also, it was a really good idea by the way. It was one of the easiest pitches to investors that I've ever done. There's nothing like it in our area. We expect that we can be fully profitable in a year."

"One more thing," he said, turning to her with a half smile. "Ever heard of delegating?"

Oh snap. "Delegating? Of course."

"You're the CEO of this company and you didn't have to run this errand."

He was right, wasn't he? But she was not exactly a typical CEO, either. "I like to have my hands in everything."

While that sounded a little sexual, surely he could see she didn't mean it that way.

"I like to have control. I want to know what's happening at all times," she said.

"Got it."

She turned onto Hill Road, the road that would take them all the way to the top of the ridge. "Is that bad?"

Of course it wasn't. She knew that and she didn't need his vote of confidence. It's just that lately she did feel a tad overwhelmed. She was one person and couldn't do everything. Not forever. But eventually this would get easier, right?

"Not at all." He braced his elbow on the frame of the window. "Where I come from, it's vitally important that someone always be in charge. Got frequently reminded of this by my CO in my early days. Otherwise you have a bunch of soldiers making different decisions and the mission isn't achieved."

"Right."

She breathed a sigh of relief. This was simply confirmation that she wasn't anal or too controlling. She just cared about her mission.

"But here's the thing. Delegating is still done if you're a CO. Or, you know, a CEO."

"I see where you're going with this."

It wasn't like her friends hadn't been after her for some time that she shouldn't make the job everything. But often, running this company didn't feel like work. When it came to spreadsheets, yeah, that was work. Seeing everything come together the way it had recently had become thrilling and addictive. Sometimes she couldn't shut off the ideas in her head, coming to her late at night when she should be sleeping.

Also, she didn't have a boyfriend to help occupy her time. There was that.

"Sam? Can I ask whether you'd take a leadership role here?"

He snorted. "Hey, I'm getting promoted already?"

"No. It's sort of off-the-books right now."

Besides, she'd noticed he was already leading. It

seemed easy for him. Might as well let him know she appreciated it.

"Might want to ask one of the other guys, too. Not sure how long I'll be sticking around."

She hadn't thought of this being a temporary stop for Sam, but what did she really know about him?

"But for now," Sam said. "I'll keep these bozos in line. You can count on me."

Chapter Six

Because the upcoming weekend would involve their first trial run, Sam found himself with a couple of days off at the end of the week.

Julian left town to meet up with an old friend in San Francisco. Michael and Ty were headed to Santa Cruz to catch some waves. Of course, he'd been invited to tag along, too, but had made excuses. Lied and said he had other plans.

He had no other plans. His plans were for some alone time. His plans were a punishing hike off trail in the heat of the day. Maybe run across some of the mountain lions native to the area. Late that morning, when he got back from the seven-mile hike, having spotted exactly zero lions, he walked down to cool, pristine Anderson Lake. It was a great day for a swim, the temps inching up into the high 70s. He'd certainly worked up a sweat. A swim sounded good.

He quickly found that he was not alone in this idea. In the distance, Jill appeared to be sunning herself on a rock, a towel on the ground nearby, her Kindle on top of it. She wore a skimpy red top that left little to the imagination. A short skirt that came to just below the thighs of those long and luscious legs.

He'd avoided her since their trip to the hardware store, always busy when she came around to check their progress. She was an intriguing woman, and the more he learned about her the more intrigued he became. But he couldn't afford to be interested in her. She was wrong for him on many levels. Sweeter than he'd realized. Someone determined, who accomplished her goals and didn't fail at them. She needed someone more like her, someone who hadn't failed at so much. Even so, he still wanted her, and talked himself out of that every night since he'd arrived.

He didn't quite understand the pull she had on him. But like he was a missile and she was the heat, he went right to her.

"Hey." He stopped on a dime right behind her.

She whipped around so fast she almost fell off the rock. "What are you doing here?"

"I work here."

She scrambled off the rock and self-consciously pulled on her skirt. "Yes, but you guys have time off since you're working all weekend."

"I went for a hike. That's not technically working."

"I thought you went surfing." She frowned. "You should relax."

Funny. He would love to relax. But he'd left "relax" in the dust years ago.

"I'm good."

"All right. Since you're here, I'm due one new thing about you."

"How did I know you were going to say that? Remember my thing was big enough to carry me through another day."

She sighed, turned away and walked toward the edge of the lake, where the water gently lapped to the shore.

He followed. "But I'm owed one thing about you."

"Seriously?"

"New day and why not? Two can play this game."

"Fine. You're right. I think I work too hard."

"Nice try. Doesn't count. I already know that. Everybody knows that."

Although he would not have guessed that to be true the night they'd met. Then, she'd given him the impression of someone who knew how to unwind. Relax and drive a man crazy. No, there was not much Jill Davis could hide from him. He'd already learned plenty without her assistance. She worked too hard, had a serious case of hero worship for her older brother and cared far too much what people thought of her. The last one was an educated guess, but he'd lay serious money down that he was right.

Still, this game was amusing, if more to find out what she'd be willing to tell him.

"Here's something about me." She blew out a breath. "I have two best friends, Carly and Zoey. You'll meet them this weekend on the trial run. Anyway, Zoey runs a pet store in town, Pimp Your Pet. And she's sort of the Pied Piper of dogs. That's to say, if you really want a Labrador, she can probably find you one."

"Great. As soon as I'm settled, I'll look her up."

"Settled?"

"If I wind up staying here in Fortune."

"Okay, but why wouldn't you stay? You have a job here."

"It's temporary, the agency said."

"Leading to permanent. I'm going to need guides."

"Wouldn't that be awkward? You and me, long-term boss and employee?"

"Not unless we let it." She put one toe in the water, then drew it back like she'd been stung by a bee.

"Cold?" He laughed.

"This lake isn't swimmable until August." She stepped back. "It's perfect for kayaking and wakeboarding. All the water sports."

He squatted and tested the water. Cold but not arctic. "It's not bad at all."

"It's got to be fifty degrees."

"Not even."

"That's pretty big talk for someone who's standing there fully clothed." Her gaze swept from his long-sleeved tee, down to his long hiking pants and boots.

She had a point.

"You probably shouldn't have said that." He grinned and kicked off his hiking boots and socks.

"What are you doing?"

"Isn't it obvious?" The shirt went next, followed by the pants, one leg at a time.

"Don't get naked!" She covered her eyes.

"Hell, no. You're not ready for that."

He walked in the lake wearing nothing but his boxer briefs. This was just what he needed to cool off. Better than a shower after a hike or run. The cold water stung and, accompanied by the warmer temps in the air, was a shock to his system. Felt like hundreds of razor blades hitting him at once. He swam several feet out and looked behind him. Jill stood at the edge, watching him, her arms crossed, head cocked.

"Isn't it freezing?"

"Nah." He dunked his head and came up as clearheaded as he thought he'd ever be around her. He wasn't going to lie. The pain helped. "Come on in if you don't believe me."

He waited. Waited for her to realize that despite this pull between them he wasn't going to be the one to act on it.

Jill stripped down to her underwear. That underwear was a matching plunging red bra and panties that seemed to cover only the essentials. He swallowed hard. She waded into the water, grimacing at turns, but pushing forward. He liked that about her a whole hell of a lot. She was tough when she had to be. Tough and brave.

She would have to be, to have approached him that night in San Francisco. He'd been in a hell of a snit until he'd looked up to see her face.

She swam to him, teeth chattering. "You're r-right. It's n-not b-bad."

"Uh-huh." His body had already become adjusted to the water, in part thanks to the rescue training he'd had during a short stint with Special Forces. "You cold?"

"N-no."

"Liar." Telling himself he'd do it for any one of his men, he rubbed down her spine and up again, creating friction and warmth. He shouldn't let her go into shock. In fact, he really should get her out of the lake.

Surprising him, she wrapped her long legs around his waist and buried her face in his neck. He went instantly hard.

"Sam."

"Yeah."

"It was one night."

"I know. One perfect night."

She pulled back to meet his gaze. "We were strangers and now…we're not."

"Is that a problem?"

"No, but this is my life. My town. You're in it and you work for me."

"It wasn't planned."

"Neither was that night. But now it's…complicated."

"Or basic chemistry." He dropped his hand to her bottom and squeezed.

She made a tiny sound in the back of her throat he found extremely gratifying. "You make it sound so simple."

He lied. "It is."

"See, I have a confession. That night…that wasn't really me you met. Okay, so it was a version of me. But I'd never… I'd never done that before. A one-night stand."

"First for me, too."

"Really?"

Her wide-eyed look of shock made him chuckle. "I'm going to pretend that didn't hurt my feelings."

She kissed his shoulder. "That did *not* hurt your feelings. But I'm sorry. It's a surprise."

"I accept that."

"But here's something new for you about me. This is going to make two things in one day. My *real* life is difficult. People depend on me. Sometimes I manage to let them down. But I'm not going to screw this—" at this she nudged her chin toward the land all around them "—up."

She managed to let people down? Somehow he doubted that. That she worried about letting others down? That he believed.

"I'm here to make sure you don't screw up."

"Thank you." She pressed her forehead to his. "But… you and me. *That* could screw things up. For me."

With no words to make his case, he kept quiet, because she was right. More than she could have known. In his current condition, he'd ruin her. Just drag her down into the dark depths with him. All her optimism and exuberance would be gone. And that would kill him.

"Unless it's just one more time," she said.

Again, he thought perhaps words were going to get in his way at this point. Especially when he liked where this was headed.

"Sam?"

Great, now he was going to have to say something that might possibly risk this. "Right there with you."

"So, you agree? One more time? Just to see if—"

"If it was a fluke."

"Right. Because maybe it was that night, or the mojitos, or the city, or the fact that we were both lonely."

He knew it was none of those things. Not for him. "Sure. We could tell ourselves that."

"Or we could find out. For sure."

Chapter Seven

From the moment Sam had stripped down to his tight boxers, Jill hadn't had a rational thought in her head. Or any thought that didn't involve her naked and under Sam as soon as humanly possible. His body was exactly as she'd remembered it. Perfect. One long, lean and muscular cord of genuine strength. The half sleeve of tattoos on one arm, winking back at her in the dappled sunlight. He walked with manly grace like he had no clue what he did to her. She wanted to lick him from his earlobe, down his flat stomach, straight to the *promised land*.

The water was icy, sure, but she was a trouper. This was a good physical challenge to her body and she needed more of those. Mind over matter. Control over her body as much as she had over her mind.

Besides, put a half-naked Sam in the water and she would surely follow.

Even right off a cliff.

Because, oh Lord, she wanted him. Maybe she could have this one thing right now because she'd been so good and worked so hard. And three years! C'mon! Just one more time with him. She'd find out that it was one of those crazy little things, like so many in her life, where a memory had grown larger than life over time. And reality could never quite match up to it. Then they'd go back to their regularly scheduled programming with no one else the wiser.

Sam's hands were everywhere he could touch her, and every inch of her skin felt singed by fiery and uncontrollable warmth. He kissed her, long and deep, his tongue warm, wild and wicked and her resolve shattered. She remembered him. *This.* Even when she'd been the one to approach him, even when the whole situation had been her idea, he took control.

Like he did now, carrying her out of the lake. The moment her skin hit air, the mix of frigid lake water and heat did something wild to her senses. That could be the only reason she lightly bit Sam's shoulder. But the reaction of sensing his muscles tense and bunch beneath her touch was more than worth it.

She shivered in a far different way than she had in the water and tightened her grip around his shoulders.

Sam stood her near the rock where she had her towel and Kindle, and threw the towel around her. Then he was digging through his knapsack. He pulled out a canister, a windbreaker, what appeared to be a nylon blanket and a Buck knife.

Her thoughts went immediately to Ryan's words. *Have all these men been checked out by the agency?* But he was an overprotective brother.

"A k-knife?"

"In case I ran across a mountain lion."

"Don't tell me you were going to k-kill it."

He quirked a brow. "Not unless I had to."

She huddled under the towel, shaking and feeling guilty for not sharing it as he squatted next to her, dripping wet. And then the nylon blanket became a small pup tent.

What the—?

"Is that a t-tent?"

"Always be prepared."

"For *camping*?"

"Or being stranded overnight, injured and unable to get help immediately. Shelter and warmth."

She was nudged inside the tent. Once there, she began to warm up and laid her damp towel over the nylon flooring of the tent. It wasn't exactly a bed at the Marriott but it would do. *Oh yes.*

Just outside the tent, Sam crouched and balanced on the balls of his feet. "Are you warm yet?"

She'd be much warmer if he joined her, but with every moment that passed she got the distinct impression that he would not.

"I think so."

"Your teeth aren't chattering anymore. I'm encouraged."

There was something wrong with this picture. He'd taken a different posture since placing her inside the tent. It seemed that his primary concern really did involve getting her warm. And nothing more. What had she missed here? Why was he suddenly backing off? Because that was exactly what he was doing. Taking two giant steps back.

Oh yeah. Because she was his boss, damn it. His sex-starved, extremely unprofessional boss.

"Can I have my clothes, please?" Might as well get dressed since there was nothing else going on in here.

A moment later, he handed them to her. Still not inside the tent with her. He didn't look the slightest bit cold out there. Maybe he'd been a penguin in another life.

Getting his message, she zippered up the tent.

"Look, Jill—"

She pulled on her skirt over wet panties. "You don't have to say anything. I'm sorry I suggested it. You're right, even one more time is a bad idea."

"I was just going to say that I don't have a condom with me."

After pulling her top back on over her wet bra, she unzipped the tent. "You have a Buck knife with you but no condom? Always be prepared, you said."

"Wasn't thinking I'd run into someone on my hike and need a condom."

She had some in her trailer. Bought them the day after seeing Sam again, which made her delusional, prepared or desperate. She was going to go with prepared.

"We could go to my trailer," she said.

It was wrong, her brain said, but her body fought back: Shut up! Three *years*!

He grinned and she almost came. "Probably not smart. All the other guys will be jealous."

Okay. Desperate and delusional it is.

But he was right. It wasn't smart. They couldn't do a fling. And one more time would be a fling. Bottom line: that night they'd had together could never be re-created. It was gone. And she obviously needed help remembering that she had to learn to want someone *available*. Someone solid and stable. Not someone who couldn't even tell her why he didn't have an emergency contact.

"You're right."

"Even if you weren't my boss, you don't need me messing up your life. And I would mess with it."

"Why? What's so wrong with you?"

He'd taken himself on a punishing hike on his day off. He plunged into ice-cold waters that she knew had to have been a stab of pain but he seemed to enjoy it. He didn't talk about his family and wasn't particularly ecstatic to reveal anything about himself. So she had a few clues that he had some issues.

Yet, she was still fascinated, which meant that maybe she had her own issues.

"Too many things to list."

"You seemed okay that night in San Francisco."

"Okay?" He cocked his head as if he didn't quite believe her. "I haven't really been okay for a while. But I'll get there."

She studied him as he collapsed the tent and quickly dressed, her heart hurting. He wouldn't want her pity but her mind immediately went to all the vets with PTSD that Ryan had worked with in the past. She quietly wondered if that was Sam, too, and knew better than to ask.

He held out his hand. "Let's get you back to your trailer."

As they hiked back, she enjoyed the quiet on the ridge. This protected land was known for the occasional wildfire, hence its name, but they hadn't had one in years. They were officially out of the drought and vegetation was growing back, little sprigs of green coming up everywhere the eye could see.

She'd achieved one of her goals. Turning this almost-forgotten ridge into something desirable again. Having a sunny and optimistic disposition hadn't always endeared her to people, including the town council, but soon the residents of Fortune were going to see what she'd done here. They'd see that no one should ever give up on a place just because it had some tough times. Or a person. It occurred to her that maybe, just maybe she could help Sam and do some good there, too.

He had issues with his parents, and no one knew better than she did how to navigate rough terrain with The Parentals. She had a black belt in the sport. But despite what she felt about her parent's lack of belief in her abilities, she'd at least always had Ryan in her corner.

When they reached her trailer, she turned to Sam. "Do you have a brother or a sister?"

"Ask me tomorrow." He grinned.

"C'mon! You almost killed me in that lake." She crossed her arms. "You owe me."

"No one forced you to follow me in."

"Sure, but you made it look fun." She threw up her hands. "All right, never mind. I'll ask you tomorrow."

She'd just put her key in the door and opened it when Sam spoke from behind her.

"You're going to give up that easy, Boots?"

She turned. *"Boots?"*

He rocked back on his heels. "Yeah. You're like a new recruit. I'll show you the ropes."

Show *her* the ropes? She was going to show *him* the ropes! Didn't he realize how badly he needed her help?

She went hands on hips. "If anything you're *my* boot."

His blue eyes narrowed. "Who followed who into the lake?"

Oh crap. She knew that would come back to haunt her. "Um…"

"Exactly."

He looked so smug and self-assured. She yanked her door open, planning to make a big show of slamming it in his face. But it stuck against several boxes of deliveries she'd had earlier in the day. Instead, she wound up fighting with the damned door to simply close it.

"Good night," Sam said from outside. "Fifty jumping jacks before bed. Takes care of the...frustration."

"And you do a hundred!" she shouted through the door while peeling off her damp clothes.

She heard him chuckle as he walked away.

Screw him. He didn't want to tell her anything about his life. Locked up tight.

She was going to help him if it killed her.

Chapter Eight

It only took Sam one night to realize what a tool he'd been. He'd had his beautiful boss alone, wearing nothing but her underwear, wet and quite willing. If the very next day he questioned every single one of the choices he'd made in the past six months, surely no one would blame him.

Point being, he'd done her a favor. She'd regret being with him, sooner rather than later. They'd both been caught up in each other, and in the raw and unplanned moment. He'd felt the pull, too. Felt the chemistry dig so deep that it took every ounce of his mental strength to turn her down. But turn her down he had.

Idiot.

He told himself it didn't matter. With what he now knew about hardworking Jill, she'd have blamed the encounter on herself and a moment of weakness. Then she would have excelled at avoiding him. Proceeded to tiptoe around him the rest of the time he was here. Oh yeah, and that was another thing. He had no idea how long he'd be in Fortune. This was supposed to be a temporary stop for him. Nothing permanent.

And, as if he needed another reason, she clearly deserved someone better than him.

Because his environment may have changed but he still woke each day in a cold sweat. Sometimes, out of the blue, a certain smell or sound would trigger a memory and he'd be in the desert again. Unable to feel his legs. Helpless. Clear and unflagging certainty that he didn't have the right to be alive and breathing oxygen wouldn't seem to leave him. Even after a long and punishing hike, and a swim in painfully cold water, the nightmares returned that same night. And yeah, good thing she wasn't lying next to him now. Good thing she wasn't here when he woke up out of breath, gasping for air. Feeling weak. Useless.

He planned to spend the next day off avoiding Jill. Turned out that wouldn't be much of a problem since he didn't see her truck the next morning. Maybe she'd gone home for a change. Good. None of the guys were back, so he had the entire hill to himself. He took another long hike, knowing this time he wouldn't run across a half-naked redhead by the lake. Near the end of the day he showered, then drove his motorcycle into town, finding himself in a saloon named the Silver Saddle. Interesting place. The bar was apparently run by a young married couple who loved country music, given the steady selection of music that piped through the speakers. There was a mechanical bull in the corner. Still, he managed only enough patience to sit still for thirty minutes nursing a beer before he had to leave. Far too noisy in there.

Back on the ridge he welcomed the quiet of the black

night and tried to turn in. But the air inside his trailer seemed oppressive and tight. Suffocating. He tossed and turned, fighting sleep. If only he could rest for a little while. But with sleep often came the nightmares. Worse was when they came before he even shut his eyes. Waking nightmares where he still heard the sounds of the explosion that hit their Humvee. Could almost smell burning flesh. Gasoline. The crushing inability to move his legs. Trapped. Unable to help. He'd had a mission and he'd failed. Nothing would ever change the fact that he'd been wrong. About everything. He folded his hands behind his neck and stared at the ceiling. Maybe what he needed was a woman. A distraction. Someone he could bury himself in. Someone he'd never see again. Someone who wouldn't ask him any more damn questions about his personal life.

Of course, he'd tried one night with Jill. Hadn't worked so well for him, had it?

He consoled himself with facts. He didn't have to stay in Fortune if this job didn't work out. There were plenty of cities all over California. If California didn't work he could move farther east. Maybe Colorado. He'd heard it was beautiful there. Even though on an intellectual level he understood that physical miles wouldn't do a damned thing to the shit going on in his head, it helped the anxiety to imagine it might work.

What wasn't going to work for him was talking about his parents to anyone, Jill included. He hadn't spoken to them since shortly after he'd enlisted. He still received the occasional email from his mother, to which he replied briefly, only giving her enough information to know he was still among the living. She didn't even know he was back in the Bay Area, and he wanted to keep it that way. William and Janet Hawker were both Berkeley University professors and conscientious war objectors. When he'd announced he'd enlisted as a US Marine, they hadn't taken it well. That was an understatement.

They'd both done everything in their power to stop him, staging an intervention with friends and some of their students. But in the end he was eighteen years old and they couldn't do a damn thing but threaten to disown him if he joined.

"Let me get this straight," Sam had said. "You're going to disown me if I serve my country?"

"Whatever it takes, son," his father had said. "I won't have you fight an illegal war."

Sam had tried to explain, but it didn't matter what his thoughts were on the subject. Didn't matter how strongly he felt about the military and how long he'd been drawn to it. Didn't matter that he'd never felt like he belonged to his two scholarly and political parents. This wasn't about politics to him, but about that fact that he and his friends had been forever changed by 9/11 and the aftermath.

He'd been in eighth grade when it happened and still remembered the sick feeling in the pit of his stomach. Watching the news coverage of the Twin Towers falling, he'd witnessed his parents truly shaken for the first time. In the weeks that followed, every one of the houses on their residential street had a US flag flying, including his home. Much like the rest of the country.

For the first time in his young life, Sam felt a connection in a way he'd never experienced before. He wanted to protect. Defend. He had a mission and a purpose that would only grow as the years passed and a sentiment that never waned.

It was at odds with all the expectations his parents had for him, and it was the way he'd make his own path. Since he was an only child, he understood their fear more than they realized. But it was still his life to give as he saw fit.

Eventually, two of his classmates, similarly driven, joined up before they were eighteen with their parents' permission. Not Sam. He'd had to wait.

In the end, his mother had wept openly after a big blowout fight that involved Sam's father telling him that if he insisted on doing this, he shouldn't bother to come back.

And he hadn't.

The next morning Sam went for an early run before the sun came up. He ran into Julian at the foot of the hill, stretching.

"Care for some company?"

"Why not." Sam didn't need company but he also didn't want to be rude. Julian was a good egg.

The first night when they'd all sat around the campfire, Julian seemed to be the one with the gift of gab. While none of them talked details, they all talked about their tours and where they'd been stationed. How many times deployed. Complained about the chow. Kept it light. That kind of thing. Turned out that Julian had been deployed to Iraq close to the time Sam had been on his last disastrous tour. Sam realized that meant Julian had also been in the thick of it.

No need for words.

They'd just started their run when Julian spoke. "Do anything on your downtime?"

"Hung out."

"Bossy Lady around, too?"

If he was prying, Julian wouldn't get anywhere with Sam.

"Nah, just me."

And the quiet. The memories. Nightmares. He'd ask Julian if it was ever the same for him, but there was always the chance that it wasn't. And Sam refused to be the weak link. With that in mind, he upped his game and easily bested Julian to the summit. They took a minute to watch the sun crest over the ridge and enjoy the breathtaking view into the valley. Orange and red tinges circling the sun.

Times like this, Sam thought he might actually beat this thing. Get on the other side of it.

They jogged back down and Sam headed to his trailer and a date with his shower.

"Hey," Julian said, bending with a stitch in his side. "You ever need to talk? Know I'm here."

"Yeah," Sam said, wiping sweat from his brow. "You bet."

It was their trial weekend before opening day and, according to Jill, they expected some of her best friends; her brother, the Sheriff, who didn't sound like a slouch; and a few former Air Force guys who operated a regional airport in town. Sam looked forward to the physical challenge the day would bring.

From a distance, he spied Jill talking to a pretty brunette, her long hair in braids. Next to her sat a dog roughly the size of a Volkswagen. Both women appeared to be engaged in conversation. Smiling and laughing. They looked normal. He wondered if he looked normal to other people. Sometimes it felt as if he was turned inside out but others looked at him as though he were a perfectly average Joe. They didn't stare and point, in other words.

As he approached, he immediately began to feel the sensual and pulsing waves of Jill's energy hitting him like tiny slices of light. Thanks to her, he was about to feel the same way on the inside as he must look on the outside. Normal.

"Morning," he said to both women.

"Hi, Sam," Jill said, no longer seeming irritated with him. "This is Zoey. Remember I told you about her?"

"The dog lady." He nodded.

That sounded weird as soon as the words came out of his mouth, even though they both laughed easily. But it wasn't the thing to say to a woman. His brain wasn't so far gone he didn't remember that.

This is why he didn't much like talking to people.

"That's me," Zoey said, as if he hadn't just insulted her. "I'm the dog lady."

She didn't look anything like a dog. Pretty, with beautiful olive skin. Italian or Hispanic maybe.

He pointed to the dog the size of a pony. "Your dog?"

"This is Boo," she said, patting the beast's head. "He's one of my rescues. Only it's difficult to place him because he needs just the right family."

"I'm sure," Sam said. "Someone with a lot of room. It must cost a lot to feed him. What does he eat? A poodle a day?"

Jill laughed but Zoey blinked and looked from him to Jill and back again. Wrong thing to say again. Wasn't he a winner these days, laying on the charm?

Do not joke with this one about animals.

"He's kidding, Z," Jill said, elbowing Zoey.

"Oh right," Zoey said with a snort. "For a minute, I didn't get it. That's funny."

It was not, but she was kind enough to pretend.

"Jill said it was okay to bring Boo with me, because he doesn't do too well when I leave him at home alone," Zoey said.

He could only imagine. Unless Zoey lived on a farm,

Boo was probably feeling a little constrained. Normally Sam would squat to pet a dog. In this case, he merely bent slightly at the waist.

"Hey, boy." Sam gave him an ear scratch.

Boo closed his eyes in apparent bliss and released a happy dog-sigh.

"Ah, yeah. That's the spot," Sam said.

"Oh, he really likes you," Zoey said.

Sam didn't miss that she went brows up, looking a little surprised. Probably because of the poodle joke. Admittedly, he was terrible at trying to be funny and he wasn't sure why Jill had laughed. He should stick to grunts.

"Sam likes Labradors," Jill said, also bending to pet Boo. "Maybe you can find him one."

"I like all dogs," Sam corrected. "But Boo here definitely needs a much bigger place than a trailer."

"Don't worry," Zoey said. "I'll find you the perfect dog. You've heard of matchmaking services for couples, right?"

He nodded, wondering where the hell she was going with this.

"That's what I do for people. Match them up with the perfect pet."

"It's a gift," Jill said. "She's our version of the dog whisperer."

"More like a pet whisperer," Zoey said. "You never know if your kindred animal could be a dog or a cat. Or maybe a parakeet. Remember, Jill, when Mrs. Robinson thought she wanted a cat? But she was totally a parakeet person."

"Oh yeah." Jill tossed that wild mane of hair. "And they're so happy together."

"Totally." Zoey cocked her head and moved her hands

in front of Sam in a circular motion. "But I'm sensing more of a feline energy from you."

Okay, so Jill's friend was a little odd. "I'll let you know when I'm ready to be, er, matched up."

"Right," Zoey said. "These things can't be rushed."

Michael, Ty and Julian joined them and introductions were made all around. Sam didn't miss that all three of them were checking out Zoey with more than a little interest. But she didn't pay much attention to anyone but the rangy-looking dude coming up the ridge. Due to his air of confidence and authority, even in plainclothes, Sam had to assume the man was Jill's brother. Though not a redhead, he definitely looked similar enough to be related.

"Ryan! You're here." Jill ran up to him. "I want you to meet the guys."

If Sam were Jill's brother, he would also want to meet all the dudes spending their days and nights with her. And then he'd want to run background checks on all of them, had the agency not already done that.

Introductions were made all around, Ryan shaking Sam's hand with impressive strength. This guy might give Sam a run for his money out here.

"Zoey." He nodded in her direction, looking at her as briefly as one might stare at the sun.

"Ryan," Zoey said, studying the ground.

Interesting.

In the next few minutes, more people arrived. The same couple who owned the Silver Saddle, Jimmy and Trish Hopkins. A couple of off-duty firefighters who were friends of Ryan. The pilots Jill had mentioned. Stone Mcallister and his wife, Emily. Matt Conner and his wife, Sarah and son Hunter. Levi Lambert, who he learned was married to one of Jill's best friends.

"Carly stayed home with Grace," he explained.

"Makes sense," Jill said. "This isn't really a place for a baby."

"I'm not sure it's a place for me," Sarah added. "But I'm here because I'm a trouper. Just ask Matt."

Her husband pulled her into a hug. "Aw. You're gonna love it."

"This gives me an opportunity to kick your ass," Stone said to Levi. "And you know I will."

"Just try it, big guy," Levi said.

Jill proceeded to welcome everyone with the speech she would give to all prospective customers. It involved her greeting, safety first and all the usual. She introduced the guides. According to her, all customers signed a release that would limit the company's liability. Probably similar to the one they'd signed as guides releasing them from liability if they broke their safety rules.

Damn. She was beautiful, sexy and smart. Lethal combo.

Everyone but Ryan, Levi and the two firefighters were coupled up, which for some odd reason filled him with a sense of relief. That relief didn't last long when he noticed one of the firefighters deeply engaged in conversation with Jill. Sam told himself they were discussing a controlled burn on a hill known for wildfires, but when the dude leaned in close and whispered something in Jill's ear that made her smile, Sam felt his gut tighten in a way he did not welcome. Only one thought flooded through him: mine.

No. Not yours, idiot. Get rid of that idea straightaway, Marine. Not. For. You.

Unfortunately, it was entirely possible that his body had not responded quickly enough to the order he'd just given it. Because, though he'd planned to turn away from the sight of the two of them flirting, he hadn't done so fast enough for her not to notice. Jill met his eyes and took a large step back from the firefighter, putting at least two feet of distance between them.

A movement that would have made "normal Sam" feel encouraged. But instead, the move disturbed him and he looked away. He had no intention of influencing her decisions. No intention of changing her life or rearranging her plans. If she wanted to flirt with a man, she had every right to do that. He just wasn't going to be able to watch it.

By the time they were ready to get going, Sam was chomping at the bit for a real challenge.

He got one.

They'd leveled the activities and Sam got assigned the highest level, which meant he had all the guys. Julian and the others had the women, for which they seemed particularly ecstatic, especially when one of them had to coax a nervous Zoey across the zip line, holding her hand.

Sam was gratified to give the men a good workout. That always meant a fun time to him so he had to assume it would be the same for these guys. He demonstrated first and set the tone as he put them through their paces. Whether hiking, rock climbing or zip-lining the guys were up to the task. Even fifteen-year-old Hunter. He was already as tall as his father and clearly as strong. To make it more fun and challenging, Sam divided them into teams. Not surprisingly, this seemed to light a fire under them. He put one of the firefighters, Stone, Matt and Hunter on one team. In the other, Jimmy, Levi, another firefighter and Ryan.

The men hurled insults at each other as "encouragement." Made Sam feel right at home. All of them were appropriately sweaty and filthy. Levi and Matt had challenged each other to see who could get to the top of the rock wall first. Just when he'd thought that Levi and Matt would come to blows and their Sheriff might have to arrest someone today, Jill joined them.

"We're breaking for lunch." Interestingly, she not only still looked fresh and clean, but like she'd just walked through a shower of sunshine and rainbows.

He on the other hand was filthy and loving it. Only thing wrong with this picture was that she should be dirty with him.

"Not fair," Sam grunted within her earshot.

"Fair is the weather, Sam."

"Uh-huh." He gathered ropes and harnesses. "You might have to get your hands dirty sometime."

"I'm aware of that," she said, her green eyes flashing. "And don't worry, I can get as dirty as the next guy. You of all people should know that."

That last part she said in a half hiss, half whisper to him. No doubt she didn't want any of her friends to know of their prior relationship. He wondered if even her girlfriends knew about them.

He wanted them to know. Hoped maybe some night after a few too many drinks she'd told her friends about a memorable night with a stranger she'd named Chris.

"I remember," he said. "Far too well."

Understatement.

Worse, now he had more than memories of an incredible physical connection. Now he saw a strong and smart woman who had plenty of friends and was obviously well liked. That would be because she was kind and loyal to her friends and family in addition to being incredibly beautiful and strong.

The guys followed Jill as she led the way to the picnic lunch she'd had set up lower on the hill. Most stopped to thank him for the best workout they'd had in years.

Ryan in particular had a strong grip as he met Sam's eyes. "Thanks. The most fun I've had in a decade."

It took Sam a minute to realize he had a straggler. Hunter, Matt's look-alike teenage son stood by gathering equipment.

"You don't have to do that," Sam said. "Chow is waiting on you. Aren't you hungry?"

"Yeah, but I'm in no hurry. There's plenty of food." He looked at the ground. "But I was wondering…can I ask you a question?"

"Something wrong?" The kid had Sam concerned. He looked far too serious for a teenager.

"No." He shook his head. "You're a Marine, right?"

"Still shows, huh?"

"My dad said something."

"Oh yeah?" He would guess half the town knew by now. Word seemed to get around in these parts. "What did he tell you?"

Hunter shoved both hands in his cargos and rocked back on his heels. "That you might be a good person for me to talk to. See, I want to be a Marine. I'm ready to sign up as soon as I graduate."

The words hit Sam harder than he wanted them to. It wasn't difficult to think back to the time he was a snot-nosed kid who knew better than anyone else.

He chose his next words carefully. "You're fifteen, right? Still have time to think about it."

"Sure, but there's not much to think about. I'm doing this."

"Your parents?"

"Well, my dad's cool with it. My mom's another story. I'm working on her."

"Uh-huh."

Wise words, chump. But yeah, Sam was so far out of

his comfort zone that he would soon need a map. But yet the kid kept talking. For a jarhead prospect, he talked too much. Then again, he was young. *A kid.* Sam remembered that passion and energy far too well.

But it wasn't his job or business to recruit anyone to the Corps. He was neither going to encourage or discourage. He was about as interested in this conversation as that pebble a few feet away in the dirt and would talk as much as the rock would. After a few minutes of listening to the kid, with appropriate grunts in all the right places, Sam was saved again by his favorite boss.

"Hunter. Here you are. Your dad's looking for you. Better get up there before lunch is all gone. We have some hungry men up there."

The kid took off at a near run, which meant maybe there was already some of the jarhead in him. After a few seconds, he noticed Jill studying him.

"Cat got your tongue?"

"What the hell does that mean?"

"It means I heard him asking you questions. You weren't very friendly."

"Maybe he needs to get used to that."

"Sam, he's just a kid. Just a few encouraging remarks, and send him on his way."

He quirked a brow. "And maybe if I had any I would give them."

She studied him a little bit more, almost like she was performing an X-ray. Yeah, he didn't like that. Didn't like the way she seemed to see inside him. It had been rather convenient that one night, when she knew exactly what he needed and why. Knew how to please him, almost like she understood the geography of his body. But he should have known that when two people had that kind of connection it went further than the physical.

Right now that amazing connection was a pain in his behind.

"Are we okay?" she asked.

"Should be asking you that question."

She studied a patch of grass. "We're okay. You were the smart one. Thanks for taking the high ground."

He wondered for a moment if he should be allowed to get away with that. If he should continue to let her think that he was this honorable man who'd done the right thing. Who had not taken advantage of the situation and the moment. She thought she knew him. But she only knew the best parts of him so far. She didn't know the animal that lived inside. While he was here, she might as well find out.

One battle at a time.

But when Jill turned to go, he simply followed her up the hill. What he needed right now, other than a clear head, was some chow.

Chapter Nine

After all her friends had left and Ryan personally spoke to each of the men, to further check them out Jill assumed—as if the agency's background checks hadn't been enough—she had a moment with her staff. She was really proud of them.

All of them.

"Thanks to you guys, our friends and family day was a great success."

She'd have everyone who attended today fill out a questionnaire with input as to what she could improve, if anything, but going by their comments today, she didn't think they'd have anything negative to report.

Maybe this would work after all.

Hard work had paid off along with a vision that she wouldn't give up on no matter what others said. And now she would have the privilege of having her parents eat their words on opening day. She didn't need their approval for success. She'd proven it. Now all she wanted was a way to get along with one grumpy and sexually frustrated Sam. Without having sex with him. Today, the waves of sensuality rolled off him and it seemed he would take her in the woods if she gave him half the chance.

Or maybe that was her.

After dismissing the men, she retired to her trailer and to one of the many Excel spreadsheets starring in her life. But within two minutes of the blinking cursor, she was on the phone with Zoey.

"So. What did you think? Now, be honest."

"Yeah," Zoey said on a sigh. "He really does peg the Chris Scale. But wow, he's just so...intense?"

Sweet Zoey. Probably didn't want to come right out and say, "holy crap, Jill what were you thinking having sex with that dude? This guy is just...scary. Yeah, drop-dead good-looking, but let's just be real here. He could have killed you." Zoey wouldn't say any of that, even if she was thinking it.

"I asked you to be honest," Jill pressed.

"Okay, okay. So maybe *intense* is another word for... scary?"

Bingo! "Thank you for being honest. There's hope for you yet."

Zoey snorted. "You're welcome. And are you sleeping with him?"

"No! We both decided that wouldn't be very professional, now would it?"

"Just be careful. You know I work with rescues."

Great. Hopefully Zoey was not getting ready to tell Jill that Sam needed rescuing. He did not. Not from her, and certainly not from anyone else, she would imagine.

"He doesn't need rescuing."

"I know. It's just that there's something about him that reminds me of…"

"What?"

"A wounded animal."

"I was going to say the big, bad wolf. Or, you know, maybe a lion."

"Hmm. I can see why you'd say that, and he does look a little bit like a cross between a wolf and a lion. But only when they've been hurt. When they're, you know, nursing their injuries. Do you remember when Boo got hurt one time? He might be big but he's the sweetest dog on the face of the Earth. But then there was the time he stepped on a nail. I tried to help him and he practically bit my head off."

"Okay… Sam is Boo in this scenario. Like he stepped on a nail or something?"

Jill did sense underneath all that oozing sexuality, which was all he'd allowed her to see, there was something else going on. She sensed the mystery of the rift with his family was just the beginning. However, she'd seen him interacting with the men easily. He might be on the serious side but she certainly didn't sense that he was in genuine pain. When he'd been with her he behaved normally, like they'd formed a baseline long ago and he felt comfortable there.

Today she'd seen firsthand what a difficult time he had relating to Hunter, who, even though a teenager, was one of the nicest people she'd met. She'd excused it, realizing despite his own experience or maybe even because of it, he might have misgivings about encouraging someone as young as Hunter to join the Marines. She wondered if he understood that whether or not Hunter joined the Marines, in the end it would not be Sam's responsibility if he did.

"Exactly," Zoey continued. "Like he's in a really bad mood. Licking his paw. In a corner."

Then again, it was just like Zoey to relate every human emotion to an animal. "Hmm. I don't see that."

Jill carefully moved to her trailer window and brought back the edge of the curtain. There was no one out in the now-black night. Seemed like the men had all gone back to their trailers, but from where she stood she could see Sam's trailer and inside it was dark.

She hung up with Zoey, asking her to check in on her pet bunny rabbit Shakira and promising to check back tomorrow. Jill took a quick shower in the barely one-person-sized unit in her trailer. She dressed in her yoga pants and a T-shirt. Then eyed the desk filled with paperwork and figured this was another night she wouldn't make it home. It didn't matter. She felt safe here on the ridge, despite the fact that Zoey believed a wounded lion lived right next door.

Jill didn't buy that. It wasn't that she hadn't expected he might have some issues. On the night they'd met, it was clear he was pretty much oblivious to the rest of the world. Hell, she'd had a bad day, too. At the time, she thought they could comfort each other. And she was pretty sure they had. Of course, she could only speak for herself, but that night had helped her forget for a little while. Helped her forget one more failed business venture, one more family dinner in which she had nothing to share. No real accomplishments to speak of.

But now he lived next door to her trailer, he worked for her, and even though she wasn't a rescuer like Zoey, of either people or dogs, she wasn't sure she could stay away. What that said about her she didn't know, but Sam didn't make himself easy to ignore. He'd been thoughtful enough to protect her from making a mistake with him on the day by the lake. That meant he'd considered more than his own physical desire. He'd thought of what it might mean for her. The action had been selfless, and in the light of the next morning she'd understood. Respect was important to her and Sam had given her that.

She grabbed her jacket and stepped outside her trailer into the black night. The lights were still out in Sam's trailer, which probably meant he was asleep. Made sense. He was such an early riser. All her guides were.

On the ridge, the only way the stars were ever covered was due to overcast skies. Tonight they winked back at her, clear and gleaming. Would it be crazy to live up here? Maybe if this business took off she could sell her place in town and build a house somewhere on this land. She had no idea how to build a house or where to begin, but Matt Conner was some kind of contractor so she'd start there.

She was in the middle of dreaming about how many rooms she'd have and where she'd put the kitchen when a large hand clamped over her mouth. Instead of attempting a muffled scream that might not get her far, she bit the offender's hand hard enough to draw blood. Rough calloused hands slipped down her arms and she was released.

"Good girl."

"Sam!"

He stood behind her, only a beam of the full moon and the ambient light from inside her trailer framing him. In the next moment, he drew his hand up to suck some blood off his finger. Mortified that she'd hurt him, she still couldn't take her eyes off the fluid moves of his tongue and finger.

"W-why did you do that? I hurt you! Let me see."

"I'm good," he said, and if she wasn't mistaken he was grinning at her in the semidarkness.

"You scared me." She went to him anyway, grabbing at his hand, which he did let her take and inspect.

"It's nothing."

She inspected his rough and calloused hand, drawing him farther into the light coming from her trailer window.

"What do you mean it's nothing? I bit you hard because I didn't know it was you. I thought it was some stranger creep who made his way up here. Do you see what you and Ryan have done to me? I'm jumpy now when men come up behind me and clamp a hand over my mouth."

She'd meant him to laugh, but he didn't. And he was right. She'd barely nicked him.

"It was a decent start. But if that were to really happen up here and none of us were around—"

"No! We're not going to discuss some possible scenario that might happen only because you were trying to... I don't know, what *were* you trying to do?"

He shrugged. "Short answer? Trying to prepare you for anything."

"And the long answer?"

He cocked his head. Studied her. "Wanted you in my arms again."

She couldn't help but bite back a smile. "That's the long answer? I think it's shorter."

"Whatever."

"Sam." She wanted to be in his arms again, too, knowing this time she wasn't going to die a horrible death. Without the sudden fear—and the biting. "We decided—"

"Pay no attention to me. I like to tease myself."

They'd actually decided, come to think of it, to see if the whole spark between them had been a happy accident. Then he'd shut her down. She understood why now and it only made him more endearing.

She let go of his hand, but he reached to thread his

fingers through hers. "I'm actually glad I ran into you. You owe me another thing about you today."

He groaned. "Not this again."

"One thing a day. That was our deal."

"Right. Because we shared all the crazy sex but we don't know each other."

"Stop stalling."

"One thing about me." He pulled her back into his arms. "I have a thing for redheads."

Her palms went flush against his chest and she decided that a little harmless flirting wasn't going to hurt anyone. "Ah. That explains why I was able to get your attention that night when the cute and flirty waitress did not."

"Nah. That would have been your nerve."

"Me?"

"You talked to me when no one else would. Even the waitress wouldn't look me in the eye while she flirted with me."

That was true. The woman had let her boobs do the talking. "Well, you sometimes give off a dangerous stay-away-from-me kind of vibe."

"You read me right, then. And you still approached me." He met her eyes. "You're brave, you know that?"

While she liked the idea of a brave and courageous Jill, it just wasn't true. A while back, she'd learned how to fake all the confidence and attitude. But brave? She didn't leave the house without makeup and her hair done. And once, she'd cried when she accidentally stepped on a spider. Not because she'd killed it, but because her bare foot had touched it. She wasn't brave so much as she was tough. Resilient. Growing up in the Davis household, she'd had to speak up to be heard above her parents' constant praise of her brother.

Her childhood illness hadn't helped. She'd been laid up in bed for an entire year of her life with a rare case of scarlet fever at age ten. Which had made team sports of any kind difficult. She'd had to fight with her overprotective parents to let her have a life.

All throughout her college life, she'd endured groping professors and classmates. She'd learned not to take shit from anybody. Which meant that she wasn't brave but persistent. Tenacious. She'd tried not to care what others thought about her. Which made her wonder why she cared what Sam thought. Obviously, she was still a work in progress.

"I like that you think I'm brave."

"What about my one thing?" He bent to press his forehead to hers.

"I'm *not* brave."

"Try again." He squeezed her hand.

"Okay, okay. Here's what I mean. I really want to do the zip line but I'm afraid. It's pretty high up. Don't get me wrong—it's exciting, and I'm going to do it. But it's pretty high up."

She released the truth in one breath. *O-kay. Hadn't really wanted to admit that.* Sexy and surly strangers in bars were one thing, but heights. People fell from heights. It was far up. And high.

Much as she'd like to think she'd come pretty far from that ten-year-old stuck in a bed for a year, she wasn't exactly an athlete.

"Let's go." He released her again and pulled on her hand. "Right now."

"Wait. Where are we going?"

She was about to remind him that he'd been the one to pull back, and he'd happened to be right. Still, maybe… She'd definitely be willing to reconsider. No one had ever accused her of being closed-minded. But he tugged her past his trailer, too.

"Do you trust me?" he asked, barely visible to her as they crossed under a tree that blocked the moonlight.

"Now that's the second time you've asked me. A girl could get a complex."

"Just checking."

He took out some kind of small pen from his cargo pants that was also a light. It lit up their path as they walked away from the trailers and farther up the hill. Toward the shed where they kept all the zip line equipment. *Wonderful.*

"No way." She stopped in her tracks. "It's dark."

They hadn't tested the night tours they'd planned yet. That particular offering was designed for the adrenaline junkie types. She was beginning to realize Sam was one. This was a bit of a problem because she was most definitely not. She had a hard time jogging.

"No kidding, Einstein. But that means you can't see how far up you are."

"Doesn't matter. I know."

The Tree Topper zip line was two hundred feet high. Eight hundred feet long. Speeds of about thirty miles per hour. She'd read the manual. Hell, she'd hired the engineers who designed it.

"This is designed so you can self-brake," he said as if he'd heard her thoughts.

"I'm aware of that."

"You can take it as fast or slow as you want. I'll hold your hand and ride next to you."

"What? So I can look weak?" She crossed her arms.

"Have it your way." He started gathering the equipment from the shed.

"I didn't say I was going to do this."

She watched as he put on a helmet and wrapped a headlight around it, climbed into the harness and slipped on rappel gloves. He brought similar equipment for her. When she didn't protest, he slipped the helmet on her head. Waited.

She stuck her tongue out.

"Nice. Very mature."

He offered her the harness and she slipped into it, trying to ignore the way he'd intentionally brushed a hand against her bottom. She pulled on the rappel gloves, which felt a size too big. There was still time to back out. Claim a sudden raging PMS headache or the need for a bathroom break. But earlier today, the only way Zoey had gone across the zip line was with Julian holding her hand all the way on a parallel line. When she'd returned she was beaming, and probably not just because Julian had asked for her phone number.

"I changed my mind. I do want you to hold my hand and I don't care who knows it."

One corner of his mouth tipped up in a smile. "No one here but you and me."

"But don't tell the guys. I want them to think of their boss as adventurous, free-spirited and...brave. You know, like you do."

"Your secret is safe with me." He fished something out of the backpack he'd thrown in the cart. "Here."

It was a flashlight. "This is going to be enough light?"

"Point it that way." He motioned with one finger.

She flipped it on and a beam of light flooded three feet in front of them. That didn't seem to be enough light for her peace of mind and she bit her lower lip in a cross between fear and exhilaration.

Together they rode in the golf cart farther up the hill to where the first tree platform sat. Jill's palms were sweaty and her heart skipped. She distracted herself by staring at Sam's profile. In the shadows, he looked more intense than normal. What was the word Zoey had used? *Scary.* No. Jill wasn't afraid of Sam and she had no idea why. He had talked her into doing something risky and thrilling. Something she'd always wanted to do. There might be fear in the action but she didn't have fear of him. Not sure why.

Once they'd reached the platform, both secured in their harnesses and locked into position, Jill remembered something vitally important. "We've only had this tested once at night by the engineers."

"Actually, I tested it myself. Forgot to tell you."

She deadpanned. "You forgot to tell me."

"That's right."

"When did you test it?"

"Last night. You'd gone home and the guys weren't back."

"You were alone up here?"

"Yeah. News flash. I'm not afraid to be alone up here, either."

"But Sam. That wasn't safe. Alone? What if you'd been hurt?" And what if she'd had the panties sued off her? She'd lose everything.

"I wasn't."

She'd recruited a bunch of former military men for this job, and it occurred to her that maybe she needed more insurance. Or a little mother hen talk with the men. Encourage them not to take too many unnecessary risks. Sam might not much care for his parents, but she'd be willing to bet her month's supply of chocolate that if something happened to him, they'd want someone to pay and pay dearly. They loved him. Who wouldn't? And they had to, right? It was in the parent contract. At least

Jill knew her parents loved her. They said so. They'd just never once told her they were proud.

Sam was staring at her. "Ready?"

Was she ready?

Hell yeah, she was ready. It was time. She'd no longer allow fear to hold her back. Tonight she didn't need anyone else to be proud of her. She was going to go ahead and be proud of herself. A year ago, when she'd first started on this venture, she could have had no indication that the road here would be quite this difficult. So many times before she'd failed in her other entrepreneurial attempts. And if she were being honest, she'd never taken a moment to celebrate all her small victories along the way. Instead, she'd plunged into the next challenge without hesitation. It helped ease the loneliness of having set up her life in a way where she hadn't made room for someone special.

She stared from Sam to the zip line. From the zip line to the forest below, which in the darkness she couldn't see. He was right—it didn't feel so high. She loved this view. The bright silvery stars. The trees all around them, dark enough to appear a shade of purple.

She was going to fly.

"I'm ready."

He held out his hand and she took it. And then they were off, gliding swiftly across the line, a little like flying. The wind whipped across her cheeks and stung her nose. She heard the *whoosh* sound of them traveling to the platform ahead, which rapidly approached. The ride was over faster than she'd imagined, and Sam deftly stopped them both at the second platform.

"Oh my god, that was amazing!" She was out of breath but in a good way.

"Yeah?" He grinned, switching them so they could return. "Now we get to go back."

He didn't have to tell her twice. This time Jill might have forgotten all about the hand-holding except that he took her hand again.

By the time they got back to the shed and put the equipment back, Jill was high from the experience and full of sparkle and zest. She'd never get to sleep now, and certainly didn't want anything to do with a spreadsheet. Given that she was beginning to see them in her nightmares, maybe she could take a much-needed break. It was still early. She could call Zoey and Carly. Maybe go dancing at the Silver Saddle. Or… Or maybe she and Sam could have sex.

Hey, she was here and he was here. She had a trailer. He had a trailer.

They were walking back to the trailers when Jill got up the nerve to ask him. "Why did you turn me down the other day? We were both here alone."

He stopped walking and she nearly ran into him. "Because I don't always make the best decisions. Even with the best of intentions."

"Now you sound like me."

"I doubt it."

"Because I remember we said one more time, just to see."

"I know. And then it occurred to me that you don't need my crap."

"What's that supposed to mean?"

"It means I'm not a very fun guy most of the time."

"Tonight was fun for me."

"Guess I have my moments."

They'd arrived at her trailer and he reached to tug on a lock of her hair. "Good night, boss. Thanks for being such a good sport."

That's it? Great. She almost felt like pouting. He was right. So mature. "Sure. Just don't test anything else without telling me first. Or at least wait until I get some more insurance."

"Roger that."

Before she stuck her tongue out again, Jill shut her trailer door. She sighed, took off her jacket and toed off her shoes. Why did it matter so much? And why did she still want him? Zoey was right. Maybe he was dangerous. He did seem to enjoy living life on the edge. Taking long hikes on his day off. Apparently hoping to meet a mountain lion. Testing and crossing boundaries. Keeping himself apart from the other guys, who'd all made friends.

She never really saw him relax. Whatever he'd been through, it had to be haunting and painful enough that he'd been affected on an intimacy level, as well.

It could also be that he didn't want *her* anymore. Maybe the boss label, and seeing her in action—let's face it, kicking ass and taking names—had been a huge turnoff. Some men were like that, after all. Didn't think women in positions of authority were sexy enough. Didn't think they should have such power. She didn't think Sam would be one of them, but it was entirely possible. What did she really know about him? Instead of working on her spreadsheets, Jill sat at her desk and started a list.

Things I know about Sam:
He likes dogs, Labradors in particular.
He takes his coffee black and hot.
He also likes cats and according to Zoey might be a cat person.
He likes redheads.
He's not close to his family.
Someone hurt him...

Did he have any siblings? Cousins? Best friends? How many times had his heart been broken? Had he ever been married? Had he ever been in love? Did he binge on Netflix? Her bet was no. Was he a fan of the Niners or the Rams? Because that could be a deal breaker. With Ryan, that is.

There was a heavy knock on her trailer door. Dropping her list, she opened her door to find Sam.

He grinned. "One more time. Is that offer still open?"

Chapter Ten

"Y-yes." Jill managed to stammer out. "Still open."

He stepped inside her trailer without another word. Suddenly the room was filled with his presence. With his heat.

"What changed your mind?" *Yes, yes.* She asked even though it could cause Sam to reevaluate. But it needed to be asked.

"Trying to fix something." He took a step toward her.

"Fix something? What are you trying to fix?"

In one swift move he stepped right into her personal space so they were practically toe to toe. "The problem I have making good decisions."

"Okay, because this…this is a good decision." She went on tiptoe and wrapped her arms around his neck as she whispered the words she wanted to be true. "Right?"

No turning back now. No regrets.

"I have a feeling it's going to be the best one I make this year. Maybe even this decade."

Jill bit her lower lip. He was giving her a tall order. Good thing she felt up to the task. She'd been waiting for this moment since she'd seen him again. *Her* Chris. He looked different now. His hair was in need of a haircut as it curled around his ears instead of a military buzz cut. A day or two's worth of beard growth dusted his chin and jawline instead of the old clean-shaven look. Her fingernails brushed against the bristle. It didn't matter anymore that he was her employee because he hadn't been the first time they'd met. And that relationship, such as it was, took precedence. It had established them.

That was her story and she was sticking to it.

He glanced at her cot. "That going to fit two?"

"Only if I sleep on top of you."

It was a small bed. He was a big man. Allowances would have to be made. Sacrifices even.

"You've got yourself a deal." His mouth grazed her jawline and lowered to her neck, causing ripples of pleasure and anticipation.

He rubbed her lower lip with his finger before he finally bent to cover her mouth with his.

Her hands fisted in his shirt because his kiss made her knees weak. His tongue tangled with hers, probing, seeking, teasing. He tasted like minty toothpaste and whiskey. So hot. The kiss got wild and out of control within seconds. When he broke the kiss, his eyes were hooded. He studied her for one long moment from underneath those long lashes.

She stared, too, because she couldn't believe this was happening again. "We have this…amazing chemistry," she said, a little dumbfounded. A little weak.

His only comment was to haul her up against his body until they were plastered against each other in a lip-lock. Hips to hips. Heart to heart. The only way this could be any better was with no clothes between them. As if he read her mind, Sam tore off his shirt and threw it to the side. She did the same, leaving on her red demi push-up bra. Some said redheads should never wear red. Jill liked to test some boundaries, too, she supposed. Lingerie boundaries.

Sam certainly didn't complain as his hot gaze took her in and seemed to like what he saw. His finger traced along the cup of her satin bra. He helped her remove it, then bent to kiss each freed nipple tenderly. But when he sucked a nipple in roughly, Jill nearly came right there and then. It had been so long since she'd been with anyone that she felt raw and new. *Helpless.* She wondered if it could be the same for him and found herself hoping. Maybe she wasn't the only one in the room that felt her bones turn liquid.

He had a beautiful and strong sinewy body. Hard. Her hands took a tour of his naked back, dropping to his steely buttock and clawing to get him closer. Sam followed suit, his hands on her behind lifting her to him until she wrapped her legs around him. He carried them both to the cot, where he lay on his back and eased her on top of him. He'd taken her quite literally and she didn't mind at all. She rather preferred being in the driver's seat.

She rose to pull off her jeans and matching red thong. He smiled from the cot, hands splayed behind his neck, enjoying her striptease.

"Hot." He dragged his teeth over his lower lip.

She helped him remove his cargo pants and he stripped down to nothing at all. He was much better, bigger and harder than she'd remembered. Leaning and reaching into her desk drawer, she pulled out the box of condoms she'd bought in a trusting moment and handed one to him. He ripped it open with his teeth. Her breath hitched as she watched him roll it on, stroking himself once. Unable to contain herself, she stroked him, too, and his eyes rolled back and closed.

He gripped her hips then and pulled her on top, thrusting into her with one long and powerful stroke. She took over, joining him in a rhythm all their own. Heat blazed a trail from the inside out making her tremble, and Jill held on to his broad shoulders for dear life. She bucked and thrust as a rising pressure built and like the tide refused to be held back. Then he slowed them both down, purposely holding back. She could feel it, and she bucked against him for more.

Jill had her answer at long last.

It wasn't the mojitos.

It wasn't San Francisco.

It was all Sam.

"Deeper, Sam. Harder. Please."

With a groan, he rolled her under him and they switched positions. She suspected he did so only to slow them down, but it did accomplish deeper. Oh yes, it did. And next it accomplished harder. Sam drove into her until they were both breathless, sweaty and delirious. Jill was on the edge, clawing her way to the top again, feeling a tsunami of sensations she couldn't restrain. She came hard, his name on her lips. Her climax milked his and with one last deep thrust, Sam followed her over.

And broke the cot.

Sam broke the flimsy cot with a little too much enthusiasm. He didn't feel good about that. Two legs, the bottom half as it turned out, no surprise, bent under their weight, laying them in a perpendicular position to the floor.

"I'll bring you my bed."

After his heart rate had toned down from cardiac event

levels and he realized what he'd done, that seemed to be the only solution.

"You…will…not. That's…for you," Jill said from underneath him.

She was still breathless even though he'd taken his weight off and braced himself above her. Her face rosy pink from exertion, stray hairs plastered to her sensual mouth, she was gorgeous and sexy rolled into one combustible package. And he felt like he'd been hit in the head with a two-by-four.

"Seriously, a bed is a luxury. I'm used to sleeping on the ground. They give the other service branches all the bunks. Marines sleep on rocks."

"I hope you're exaggerating." She blew out a breath and smiled.

Still under him, now squeezing his biceps. Yeah, he couldn't seem to move. Not because he was too tired or worn-out, but because her shoulders were so soft and lickable. Her neck was creamy and smelled like flowers. And he couldn't seem to move off her.

Instead, he bent down to kiss her neck and smell again. "Guess pretending to sleep on top of each other was maybe not such a good idea."

Her legs, still wrapped around his back, shivered at his touch. Her stomach tightened. He could feel every inch of her respond to him and it was damned addictive.

"Don't worry about the cot. It was cheap anyway, and remember, I don't usually sleep here."

He tugged her lower lip. "So I've done you a favor. No more late work nights and no more sleeping here."

"Right."

At least it would be comforting knowing she wasn't in here working late. It might relieve some of the temptation to invite himself over again and break another piece of her furniture. God knew he was great at breaking things.

Families, friendships, promises.

"But what about tonight?"

"Maybe I'll drive home." She sighed and arched her back.

That was his cue. "I should go."

He forced himself to move, clean them both up, put his clothes back on. His pants, anyway. Mission accomplished. Time to get the hell out of here.

"Do you *have* to go?"

He gave her a hand up and she rose from the cot with one end now level with the floor.

"I broke your bed. Do you really want to find out what else I might break?"

"Yes, actually."

She was still quite naked. This disturbed him more than he could say. In no rush to dress, she threw her long-sleeved shirt on and nothing else. Unfortunately her shirt barely came to her hips.

"I'll never look at one of these cots in the same way again. If that's what it takes to break one, I'm all over it."

"You want to break some more cots?" He couldn't help but feel a smile tugging at his lips.

"If it's always that much fun." She met his gaze. "Want to stay?"

No. What he wanted to do was go. He was itchy and antsy again, his skin too tight around his bones. The trailer too small. But she stood literally bare-assed naked having no inhibitions about this fact whatsoever and that got to him. It was easy for her, he decided. Easy to show him who she was. Someone beautiful and strong and capable. She didn't need him. She didn't need anyone. It was possibly the most attractive quality about her.

"Is this your underhanded way of getting one more thing out of me? One a day. We agreed."

She pulled on her panties, which wasn't as helpful as it should have been. "Absolutely. Don't tell me anything else. I forbid it."

"Reverse psychology?" He quirked a brow. "Nice one."

"Ha. As if I would try something so obvious." She walked to the sink of the small kitchenette and bent under the cabinet, coming up with a bottle of scotch.

"You think if I drink enough I'll spill my guts?"

"No, I think maybe if I drink enough I might be able to figure out what happened tonight." She glanced at the broken cot.

"You need a recap?"

She poured into two shot glasses. Slammed hers down and didn't even wince. Da-yum, this was his kind of girl. One more thing he didn't know about her. Girl could swallow her scotch. He did the same with his shot and set it down on the countertop.

"Is this going to work? Tell me honestly and don't hold back."

She waved around the trailer, and by "this" he assumed she meant the park and not their, uh, relationship. They didn't have one even if for a moment he'd allowed himself to consider it. He allowed himself to want more. She was so beautiful, smart and so loving. But how could he take care of anyone else when he could barely take care of himself?

"I predict great success and all this without a crystal ball." He stepped next to her and poured himself another shot. "Why? What are you worried about?"

"This is just all so big and the bigger they are the harder they fall. Everyone in town has heard about the venture and most didn't think I could pull it off. The city council already hates me for bringing in more traffic. More people from all over the Bay Area coming into Fortune. They can't get as much tax revenue from me, you know. I'm not a housing development. So if I'm a flop, I'm going to be a spectacular flop."

"Not going to be a flop."

"Good, because my parents would love that."

He kept quiet, eyeing her carefully, letting her talk. She seemed to enjoy doing all of the talking and he found he didn't mind listening.

"I was supposed to do corporate America and the *safe* thing. It wasn't me, but they didn't seem to care. They pretty much wished I'd do anything else but this. Not supportive, in other words." She slammed another shot.

He quirked a brow, slid a look at the shot, then back to her. She ignored him. "But they're coming to the opening, right?"

No matter what other people said about their parents, Sam found them to be hollow complaints in the end. He didn't know anyone else who'd been basically disowned so his perspective was probably skewed.

"Nope."

This surprised him. Jill had been raised in the land of helicopter parenting. Silicon Valley parents were not known for their absentee ways. Had someone forgotten to give them the memo?

"To them, this isn't a big deal at all. They'll be in Paris." She served him another shot, which he did not take. "Who am I kidding? I'm sure I'd be in Paris if I had the chance."

"No. You wouldn't."

She slid him a look of defiance that softened a little when she met his eyes. "You're right. Screw Paris when we've got the ridge."

"I wouldn't go that far." He went ahead and took that shot. "But I understand what it's like to have parents who are less than supportive of what you choose to do with your life."

Her eyes widened. Yeah, he got that a lot. Who didn't support their son when it seemed all of America did? When he'd been stateside, his money wasn't any good in bars. Drinks on the house. Keep 'em coming. A clap on the back. Thank you for your service, son. But not his parents. They opposed both war and the military. He'd been the crack that tore through their happy little progressive family because he didn't go along with their rule book. Because he had his own mind and wanted to find his path.

"Really?"

"Not too popular around the home front."

"And where is that home front…exactly?"

"Berkeley. That's where I should have gone to school had I not signed up when I turned eighteen."

"Oh. That's…rough."

"You know a lot about me now. You know why my parents are not my emergency contacts. They don't want to be."

She eyed him with a look of concern and outright pity that he did not appreciate.

"Don't," he ordered.

"Don't what?"

"Do not feel sorry for me. Just don't do it."

"It's *compassion*. I don't like pity, either, believe me. For a year of my life, everyone in my family treated me like an invalid. It made me sad and then it made me so. Damn. Mad."

He squinted, not comprehending. "Why would they treat you like an invalid?"

"I got very sick with scarlet fever. Ironic, huh? A redhead with *scarlet* fever. Some kids wind up with permanent damage to the heart, though it's rare. I lost a year of school, and my parents were worried. For good reason, I know, but it got suffocating. I got attention for all the wrong reasons. There's nothing I hate more than feeling helpless and weak. They have always encouraged me to use my brain instead of my body. Which, you know, could give out or something." She rolled her eyes. "I got my education, but when I didn't want to do the corporate thing they turned their worry for me into disappointment. Much better, right?"

"But you're okay now?" He couldn't help asking considering the workout he'd just given her. "Your heart?"

She took another shot. "Yes, I'm okay. Clean bill of health."

"Good."

Her eyes dipped to his chest as if she'd just now noticed he'd dressed, all except for the shirt. Which meant… Hell, he didn't know what it meant. He was in uncharted territory again. Uncomfortable. Because when he walked out that door, this wasn't over like last time. It couldn't be. He didn't understand why, but he didn't want this to be over. Not yet. But the one thing he understood, the only thing that brought him comfort now, was the thumping sound of his heart rate escalating. A rush of adrenaline pumped through him and he felt alive. Useful.

She stepped toward him. One finger traced a line from his pec down to his abs.

He grasped her wrist. "Careful."

Her eyes flashed with a hint of annoyance as she glared at the hand wrapped around her wrist. "Or…?"

"Or this one more time becomes two more times." Her pulse quickened under his fingers and the rush he felt from that was unexpected but welcome.

"I don't have a problem with that. Do you?"

Hell, lack of a bed had never stopped him before. "Not one."

Gripping her hips, he lifted her to the small kitchen counter and stepped between her thighs.

"Don't let me break this counter."

Chapter Eleven

When Jill woke the next morning, she was on her stomach, snuggled among blankets and pillows, unable to move from her soft, warm spot on the... On the floor? She went up on one elbow and forced her other eye open as memories of last night came back to her in slow percolating waves.

Oh, baby.

She rolled to her back. Last night, she and Sam had broken her cot. Broken it! There had been a little drinking afterward—mostly on her part, come to think of it—and then the kitchen counter had come in handy. Next, she'd found it was possible to fit two people in her tiny shower stall. But just barely and only if those two people didn't mind being connected at the hip. Later, Sam had separated the bed's frame from the cushion part and laid it on the floor with some of his blankets and pillows. He'd offered once more to move his bed and when she'd refused yet again, he'd pulled her into his arms on the floor.

Where she'd slept some of the best sleep she'd had in weeks. The sleep of babies and pets. The slumber of those who didn't worry about anything at all. And she happened to be sore in the best way possible. Not gym sore. Sex sore. Sam wasn't on the floor next to her, which didn't surprise her. The last time they'd done this one-shot deal, she'd been the one to sneak out. It was his hotel room and she'd left him sated, satisfied and asleep, one brawny arm thrown over his face.

Who in the world didn't support their son when he chose to serve in the military? She'd never heard of such a thing. Jill was about as patriotic a person as they came and no matter what she thought of the conflicts, she would never turn against the men and women who simply wanted to serve their country. It was difficult to believe anyone would. Her parents hadn't been thrilled at the prospect of Ryan entering the service, but they'd gone along with it when he went to the Academy first. Probably thinking that he'd avoid combat being an officer. Not smart enough to realize Ryan would do no such thing. But they'd supported him no matter what. Obviously, he was their favorite.

Damn! She'd forgotten to ask Sam if he was an only child. Still, that was no excuse. Maybe she'd ask Sam if he'd like to invite his parents to the grand opening. A way to mend fences and such. Then again, she should stay out of it. Sometimes she was far too optimistic and got a bit annoying. It was her weak spot. She could almost hear Ryan telling her in no uncertain terms that regardless of how good her intentions might be, she didn't understand what a soldier had been through. All the battle scars that changed who they were. This was a complicated situation. She should stay out of it.

But she couldn't understand disowning a son because

he'd gone against his parents' wishes to do something as noble as serve his country. They'd obviously done so only to stop him from going, and when that hadn't worked they were stuck. Once a person took the tough love stance there was no backing down without losing face. Go back on your word, or lose contact with your son. A heartbreaking choice.

There was a knocking on her trailer door and the sound of a voice she recognized far too well. "You must be in there because I see your truck."

Oh crap. *Ryan*. She so did not want him to see the broken cot. Maybe he wouldn't notice? But of course he would! He was the Sheriff, for the love of coffee.

"I'll be right there." She jumped up and dressed quickly, throwing on yesterday's clothes. Jeans. A Wildfire Ridge polo.

She stepped outside before Ryan could even think about coming inside the trailer.

Her big brother was holding two coffees from The Drip. "Morning, sleep monster."

"Oh my god, this is why I love you so much." She accepted the cup and drank deeply of her favorite liquid on the planet.

It helped her form complete sentences and do simple math before noon.

"Did you forget?" Ryan asked, glancing down at her clothes.

"I know, I know. You don't like me sleeping up here, but it got late and there was a spreadsheet." And some scotch and other fun stuff, but let's not go there.

"No, Jilly," her brother said with great patience, "our meeting with the mayor is this morning."

"No!"

This morning? Yes, this morning! How could she have forgotten? It was so unlike her to forget her appointments.

"You got any other clothes in there?" Ryan nodded toward her trailer.

"Nothing any better than this."

She looked down at her rumpled jeans and company polo. As a joke, which the guys had found hilarious, she'd had her own embroidered with Bossy Lady. Not city hall humor. Besides, she had planned to wear her red power suit complete with black pumps that clickety-clacked so everyone would know she was coming down the hall. So they could get all ready for her awesomeness.

She did not look awesome.

Ryan glanced at his wristwatch. "Well, come on. You forced me to come to this meeting with you, remember? Moral support. We've got to get down the hill and to the meeting."

"Are you crazy? How can I go like this?"

"I don't want to reschedule. And the mayor is a busy man, not to mention this is an election year." Ryan scowled.

"No. We can reschedule."

"He won't care. You're running extreme sport events, not the Miss America campaign."

But she was the CEO of this company. *Her* company. "Give me a minute."

As quickly as she could manage without her second cup of coffee, Jill showered and dressed again. She reapplied her makeup and pulled her wild hair into a ponytail. She'd explain to the mayor she'd been busy on the ridge and didn't have time to go home and change. She'd think of something. When she emerged, Ryan was talking to Sam. *Great.* She would have to act business as usual after the second most erotic night of her life.

"See you later! We have a meeting." She hopped into Ryan's Jeep even before he did.

When he finally eased into the driver's seat, he gave her a puzzled look. "You take thirty minutes to get ready and you can't take two to say good morning to your employee?"

"I said good morning!" Wait. No, she didn't. Anyway. "We're in a hurry."

Besides, she was afraid that her feelings would show all over her face and in her eyes. The afterglow. It was too soon. Once she had a few more minutes and a few more ounces of coffee, she would manage to hide her thoughts from Sam and from everyone else.

He'd really rocked her world last night. She'd so wanted San Francisco to be a onetime thing because it would have made her life easier. They could have just chalked it up to loneliness or the low light and ambience of the bar or the… Anything. But no, it *had* to be Sam. She had this thing for him that was not going away. He was not just attractive, he'd been through so much and still he had the courage to keep moving forward. Yes, she wanted him. But the worst news of all was that she had started to need him.

The most unavailable man on the planet.

"What were you two talking about?" Jill asked, trying to appear disinterested by looking out the window. "Did he mention me at all?"

Ryan cocked his head and gave her a sideways look. "Did he *mention* you?"

"What I meant is did he mention that he loves working for me? That I'm the best boss he's ever had and he'd never in a million years think of quitting such a cushy gig."

"Yeah, I think he said all of those things." Ryan

smirked. "You don't have a thing for him, do you? Because that would be stupid and you're far from stupid."

"Don't read anything into it. I'm just...wondering how I'm doing as a boss."

"Ah, okay. What we did discuss is you working too much and sleeping in your trailer. He assured me that it wasn't going to happen anymore."

At that, Jill was certain her entire face was the bright color of a strawberry. She sank a little in her seat and stopped talking. Ryan drove them into downtown Fortune and the city hall building on Main Street near the library.

Fortune was a smaller town, or used to be, and Mayor Mark Coggins was actually someone that they'd all gone to school with. He had been a couple of years ahead of Ryan. Mark had served many years on the city council where he merely got a stipend but now he was a bona fide government employee.

Mark and Ryan exchanged pleasantries and then they went straight to business. If Mark had any comments about her outfit, he sure didn't mention them. Didn't even blink twice. He was concerned about the environmental impact study. Which they'd done a year ago.

She took a deep breath. "Mark, we couldn't even move forward without the study. Is there a problem?"

"Not a problem. Just a concern from one of the residents."

A little late, Jill resisted saying. She'd jumped through hoops for the residents for what felt like ten years instead of approximately two. Surely she'd aged at least ten years in that time. Accounting could do that to a girl.

She gritted her teeth and smiled as Ryan had advised her to do. "I'm always available for residents who want to voice any concerns."

"Oh good. I love to hear that." Mark shuffled some papers on his huge mahogany desk that her tax dollars paid for. "We can take care of this at the next council meeting. I'll put you on the docket."

Jill glared at Ryan sitting next to her, staring straight ahead and ignoring her wrath. He might have warned her. Only he knew how much she hated those stuffy meetings. He had to attend them, of course, but she thought she was done with all that.

"Wonderful." She leaned forward. "Can you just give me a hint as to what the concern might be? We are only a couple of weeks away from our opening day."

Noise level? She'd had that checked and they were far enough away that most residents wouldn't hear them. *Environmental impact?* They were actually helping to bring back the ridge from some of the fires it had endured over the years. *Traffic?* Not much she could do about that, but she'd provided only enough parking so that they could obtain some revenue from tickets. Ryan hated that idea as much as she did.

"It's some kind of wildflower."

"Wildflower?"

"Yes, apparently it's indigenous to the area." He shuffled papers on his desk, his brow furrowed. "Here's the formal complaint."

"We had the study and no one mentioned a wildflower." Her throat tightened as she scanned the complaint, and her voice went up into the squeaky register Mom referred to as "whining."

"I know, I know, but there it is." Mark threw up his hands. "Honestly? Some days I hate my job."

And some days Jill wanted to go back to bed and start over.

On the way back from the meeting, Jill had Ryan drop her off at Carly's. She had potted flowers on her front porch so she had to know something about flowers, right? Maybe she could help. Jill wouldn't know a rosebush from a toothbrush. Okay, she was exaggerating. But she'd never exactly been little miss homemaker.

Carly answered the front door wearing a beautiful blue silk blouse complete with a ruby pendant showcased on a simple gold necklace. Above the waist, she was the picture of elegance and style. Below the waist, she wore yoga pants and Tazmanian Devil slippers. Her work clothes. Carly worked from home and the thing about that was she might be home but she was hardly ever available.

Still, all Jill wanted was to look in her garden for wildflowers and get some advice.

"What's up?"

"Do you have a minute?"

"Sure, I just finished a Skype meeting." Carly moved and let Jill inside.

"Levi?" Her pilot husband worked odd hours, and one never knew.

"At the airport."

"The baby?"

Grace was adorable, no doubt, but she was a handful.

"At the sitter's."

Jill took a deep breath, convinced she'd have Carly's undivided attention. "I have a wicked serious problem."

"Oh good. Because you caught me on my wicked serious problem day."

"Do you have any special flowers in your garden?" Jill headed toward the backyard.

"Why? You need some?"

"Actually, I need to know what you would do if you had a super special flower you wouldn't want anyone to get to."

"Jill, what on earth are you talking about?"

Jill explained the grim wildflower situation.

"I'm going to get on top of this immediately. Find the wildflower, and solve the problem before it even *becomes* a problem."

"Seriously? When you might not even have anything to worry about?"

"I have a lot to worry about! Someone wants to delay my opening."

"You're always doing this. Always worrying about stuff before it's even happened. You don't know that it's going to be an issue yet."

Her friends were so clueless, living their simple lives with their husbands, babies and dogs. Meanwhile she was trying to swim upstream like a salmon.

"Remember when they found that endangered butterfly on El Toro Hill? They couldn't build the high school there for six years. Six years, Carly!"

"Well, that's different. It was a butterfly. They're so pretty."

Jill plopped down on the couch in Carly's living room, out of steam. It had been a busy morning after a sexually charged and sleep-deprived night. She hadn't had nearly enough coffee yet to be solving problems.

"I'm just tired of all the obstacles. You know better than anyone I've been ducking all the flame torches the concerned residents have thrown my way. Three years of them. Traffic. Noise. Blight. And of course, did I mention traffic? And just when I think I'm finished taking care of every possible objection on planet Earth, there's another one."

"You're so close. It's going to happen."

"Remind me again why I did this?"

"Because there are one too many inns and B and Bs in the area, and you wanted something special."

"Something big. Life changing."

"There's nothing like it in our area." Carly sat beside Jill. "And when you came up with the idea to hire veterans as guides...that was brilliant. A stroke of genius."

"Thanks."

But after so many failed ventures, she was bound to eventually find success. It was just a matter of odds, and she'd finally beaten them.

"So. Levi had a great time."

"I'm glad."

"And?" Carly was obviously waiting for something, and Jill could guess what that something was.

Jill folded like a blanket. "I slept with Sam! Why the interrogation?"

"Actually, I was going to ask if Zoey followed Ryan around all day, but this is a whole lot better. Do go on, please."

"It was just once. That's all." Guilt flooded her. She was such a bad boss. "We were both curious."

"That's totally understandable."

"Wow, you are being way too easy on me."

"Or maybe you're way too hard on yourself." Carly grinned. "I mean, I haven't seen him yet but I got the full report from Zoey."

"Yes, he really is something to see. But that doesn't excuse my lack of self-control."

"What did you do? Attack him and tie him up?"

"No! It was totally mutual."

"That's what I thought."

If only it were that simple. "I have a problem. I really *like* him."

"Yeah?"

"Even more than I thought I did. He's...he's just so..."

Carly leaned forward.

Jill tried to find words and continued to stammer. "He's…"

"I think I get it."

"But I haven't said anything."

"Oh, yes you have."

But Jill was still trying to find the right words. Sam had an indefinable quality to him that pulled her in. He was also a good listener. She couldn't remember the last time a guy had really cared enough to listen to her go on and on. With Sam, she tried to tell herself that he had the same investment she did in the success of the park. At the same time, that alone didn't ring true. Unless she was misreading him, he genuinely seemed to care.

She could get used to that.

"Any advice for me? I mean, what did you and Levi do after that first time? Did you feel terribly guilty?"

"In my case, it was a little different because Levi had a child. I knew I couldn't just have a fling with him. I worried that I'd hurt him and Grace both if it didn't work out between us."

And Jill worried despite all her best intentions she'd hurt a man who'd already been hurt enough. By the world. By his family. She had no idea how deep those wounds went, because the family issue was the only one she knew about. There had to be so much more and he wasn't talking.

"He's…damaged. And I don't want to make it worse."

"Then don't. Just be that soft place for him. Listen to him."

"He doesn't like to talk about his personal life. I've had to drag stuff out of him." Jill stood to go. Visiting time was over and she had to get back to the ridge. "I'm going to keep my hands off him from now on. I'll be his friend. I don't want it to get weird between us."

"What are you going to do if he wants more?"

It could be a problem. Sam trying to steal a kiss when no one else was looking. Maybe cop a feel here and there. Sneak into her trailer for a nooner. Yes, it could work out to be *quite* an issue.

Frankly, that would be one problem she'd love to have.

Chapter Twelve

Sam was in deep trouble.

Jill was not only beautiful, kind, loyal and brave, he was beginning to believe he couldn't walk away from what they'd started. It wouldn't be the same as the first time. This time they couldn't easily walk away from each other. But rather than regret that, he was grateful. She couldn't get away from him. It wouldn't be easy to walk away, and damn if he would make it simple.

Like her, he knew a little about overcoming physical odds though he hadn't opened up to her like she had to him. After the explosion, some of the doctors thought he'd never walk again. The spinal surgery he'd had carried a risk of permanent paralysis or death, but he'd rolled the dice and taken it. Do or die. He'd had the surgery. Some could live out long and fruitful lives in a chair. Sam didn't think he could be one of them.

The rehabilitation had been what nearly killed him. He

could still see the kind and compassionate looks on the nurses' faces. They'd written him off and felt sorry for him, and grateful for his sacrifice. Once he'd accidentally heard a nurse say it was too bad he was so young. Having seen so many soldiers come through with injuries they'd never overcome, they obviously expected the same out of him.

He hated their pity because he'd been long ago prepared to die for his country. But losing the ability to walk was a different scenario. He'd feel the anger and hostility course through him with every compassionate glance. Hated the assumptions they'd made about him.

Jill hated pity as much as he did, and that knowledge settled deep in him. She understood.

This morning, he'd taken his leave of her before anyone could suspect they'd spent the better part of a night together. It hadn't been easy. She'd looked soft and vulnerable lying fully naked on the faux bed he'd fashioned out of pillows and blankets. He'd skimmed his hand down her spine to the small of her back and silently cursed at his idiocy. How could he have ever entertained the idea that once more could get her out of his system? One more time had done the opposite. It had firmly established one true reality. She was not someone he'd ever be able to forget.

So there was that.

Back in his trailer, he'd showered, made coffee and waited for the sun to come up. No way could he sleep. He was too wound up to relax. While he waited for dawn, he went over some of the ideas he'd had for the park. Ideas to expand the offerings to excursions to Lake Tahoe for snowshoeing and skiing. He outlined the possible logistics of such an endeavor. Sometimes he couldn't shut his brain off. Today he and the other guides had plans for a hike they'd scope out before the opening. This one was a higher level, more switchbacks and inclines, and climbing to the summit. They were going to rate the hike, hoping it would rate as moderate to extreme. They wouldn't know for certain until they tried.

He'd heard the cruiser rolling up the hill a couple of hours later and realized he'd lost track of time. Since Jill's trailer was next to his, he heard the loud knocking and Ryan calling for Jill. He felt a little guilty as he overheard snippets of their conversation. She'd obviously forgotten an appointment. Sam wanted to believe that was because he'd kept her otherwise entertained for most of the night and wiped her out. Because of who he was at heart, he'd treated the sex last night like a competitive sport. He had every intention of making himself and last night as unforgettable as the first time and now he felt an odd pinch in his chest realizing he'd intervened in her seemingly carefully arranged life. He wanted to do just that—muss up her hair, bruise her lips, leave behind a love bite or two.

When it had become clear Ryan had not been invited inside her trailer and was instead waiting outside his cruiser, Sam made the decision to join him. While he wasn't Mr. Social, Ryan Davis had something in common with Sam. He also apparently had a medal from his time in the service. Sam's was a Purple Heart and he talked about it about as much as it sounded like Sheriff Davis did. Not at all.

Sam didn't know anyone still fogging up a mirror who did. Getting a medal for being alive while your friends were dead was particularly stunning.

"Hey." Sam greeted Ryan with a chin lift.

Ryan was tall and rangy and looked more like a former soldier than any officer he'd ever met, and yet there was the sense of authority surrounding him, too. Whether from his previous life or his new life as Sheriff, Sam didn't know.

Ryan's head had been bent down studying his phone, but he rose and met Sam's eyes. "How you doing?"

Sam nodded. "Anything I can do to help?"

"Waiting for Jill." He held up his phone. "We're late for a meeting. It's not like her to forget. Must be everything she's taken on."

"Doing what I can to relieve the workload."

"Don't doubt it." Ryan seemed to hesitate, then spoke. "Actually, you might be able to help when she gets back from this meeting with the mayor."

"Trouble?"

"Afraid so. Have a feeling she's not going to be thrilled, I can tell you that much."

"How can I help?"

"Remind her it's not the end of the world as we know it? I noticed you've taken lead around here and I appreciate that. She needs a right-hand man around here even if she refuses to admit it."

"Got it."

Just then Jill flew out of the trailer, the door nearly flying off its hinges. Her gaze briefly locked with his before she looked away and practically threw herself in the front seat of the cruiser.

"Huh." Ryan stared from Sam to Jill and back again. He nodded briskly. "See you around."

Going by the furrowed brow, Sam guessed that Sheriff Davis had his suspicions about Jill and Sam. He couldn't blame him. Her clear avoidance of him was too calculated and couldn't have been more obvious.

Later that afternoon on the ridge after her meeting with the mayor, Jill squatted in a field to admire the bright yellow flowers that decorated a part of the hill slowly returning to life. She petted the flower gently, admiring its soft ruffly edges. She took a photo with her phone so she could later do an image search and identify it.

"How could something so beautiful be so much trouble and what did I ever do to you?"

It was a Mimulus. Had to be. This was the wildflower that the concerned resident had mentioned. There weren't many flowers left on the ridge, not even poppies, their state flower, most having been obliterated in previous fires. But the beautiful Mimulus had come back. To haunt Jill, of course. She didn't see the problem. Surely the wildflower could coexist with a bunch of extreme sports enthusiasts. Surely this wildflower appreciated hot guys. They wouldn't step on the flowers. What if she swore an oath to that fact?

She couldn't allow anything to slow down their opening at this point. That would be a huge failure. She'd done so much advertising and spent so much of their promotional budget banking on their opening date. Why couldn't anyone have mentioned this to her sooner?

Jill could just hear her father right now: *Forewarned is forearmed. Always do your research. Confirm your first and secondary sources. For God's sake, don't Google it. Are you ever going to listen to me? Jill Davis, this is your father speaking!*

"Get a room."

"Huh?" Jill rose and turned to the sound of a smooth-as-whiskey voice.

Sam grinned. "You two look like you'll be pretty happy together. Even if you are a different species."

"Meet Ms. Wildflower, my nemesis."

"Looks harmless to me."

"Shows how much you know!"

He quirked a brow. "How is this flower hurting you?"

"It's not," she huffed. "But I might be hurting it. I found out this morning that I have to get through one more snooze fest of a city council meeting because a resident is concerned about a wildflower on the ridge that's indigenous to the area. We had an environmental study and no one mentioned it."

"And this is the flower?"

"You see any others around here?" She shoved past him. "It's called Wildfire Ridge for a reason."

He followed her, steps behind her. "What does this mean? You can't open?"

"No one's going to stop me from opening. But it means lots of meetings and reports and maybe…delaying our opening."

This didn't seem to faze him in the slightest. "And?"

"And that wasn't the plan!"

"Move to Plan B, babe."

"Move to Plan B, he says. Move to Plan B."

"Is there an echo here? Calm down. We can work this out."

He smiled and stepped into her personal space. One hand wrapped around the nape of her neck. Nervous, she did her usual yammering when a really hot guy was this close. A super hot guy that she had growing feelings for.

"I've sunk thousands of dollars into marketing with our opening date. I'd have to spend more money changing everything. All the graphics and ads. We're booked solid for six months. And I've already invited so many people to our grand opening." She took a breath, and then a chance. "I had hoped you would invite your parents to come. But not until I'm sure of the exact date."

His hand came down and he took a step back. "Why would I invite them?"

"Because, Sam, they were wrong."

The expression that crossed his face wasn't the one she'd wanted to see. His jaw tightened and his eyes narrowed. "Don't. Don't do this. You're feeling sorry for me. I didn't ask you to fix me."

"I'm not trying to fix you." She pointed to him. "That was you. *You* said you were trying to fix your bad decisions."

"This isn't about me." He shook his head. "You say you don't care whether your parents come to the grand opening. You think you don't care whether they approve of what you've done here. But you do."

"That's not true. I don't need anyone's approval, least of all theirs."

"Then why did you take on such a huge venture? You don't take on something as public as this is if you're not looking to impress someone."

He'd managed to turn this all around on her, but she didn't want to hear this. Her parents had nothing to do with her choices. Stepping away from him, she wandered down a trail.

"You don't know me like you think you do. You're wrong."

"I'm wrong?" He followed her. "It's clear that your big brother is your hero. And good choice, by the way. But I get that he may have stolen some of your thunder."

"Ryan didn't... Okay, look. I'm not talking about this."

She hiked farther down the path hoping he'd catch the hint she'd just pitched him and leave her alone. She liked stewing in denial on her own. Her trail of denial was an expert-rated hike and she could do it with her eyes closed.

But he was still following. The ground was so dry that she lost her footing a little and slid down part of the trail, recovering her balance by grabbing onto a sturdy shrub. "God, I hope you're not a special snowflake, too."

"You talking to a shrub now?"

"I'm not talking to anyone right now. Especially not you."

He was right, damn it. Being up close and personal with Sam, who truly didn't need anyone's approval, forced her to see it clearly. He wasn't faking this. It was clear he didn't care. But she'd wanted her parent's approval far too much for a badass such as herself. And okay, maybe all the encouraging self-talk hadn't helped. Her theory was "fake it till you make it." She should be past wanting approval from anyone, but saying it to herself and anyone who listened didn't make it true.

She wasn't sure how she felt about Sam reading her so clearly. Not just seeing right through her, either, but calling her on it, too. Ryan probably suspected too, but he hadn't confronted her. He hadn't been right in her face about it like Sam had. He reminded her of herself. It was exactly what she did with her friends and with anyone she truly cared about. Try to get them to acknowledge the elephant in the room.

Even though she'd appreciate some approval sometime this millennium, that's not why she'd put her heart into this project. Sam was right that she could have chosen many other businesses that weren't this public but she was tired of working for something that didn't have her whole heart. This idea had gripped her from day one and she just couldn't let go despite the all-consuming work and time involved.

She continued to walk the trail leaving Sam in the dust. But he was a hell of a lot more sure-footed than she and in no time at all he'd cut through the trail and was ahead of her.

He stood before her, those strong arms folded across his chest, and the hint of a smile on his sensual mouth.

She'd never seen a man look better in a pair of tan cargo pants and a T-shirt. Said T-shirt strained against his arm candy biceps, which had something to do with it. Sam wasn't wearing the T-shirt. The shirt was wearing him.

"Hey, I'm sorry. Let me make you a deal." His gaze was full of a mix of sensuality and compassion that shocked her to the core. "You stay out of my personal business and I'll always have your back."

"What?" This man of all people was going to have her back? Not possible.

He took another step forward and his hands slipped to her waist. "Look. You've done a great thing here. I know it, and every one of the men know it. Your brother knows it. Soon the whole damn town is going to know it. What you need to do is stop caring so much what your parents, or anyone else, thinks. Stop trying to show them that your version of you is better than their version."

Since he'd done such a good job of it himself, he might figure it should be that easy for everyone. "Oh really. Is *that* all?"

He chuckled. "I didn't say it would be easy. But it has to be easier knowing you're right."

"What does that mean?" That sounded odd. "Knowing I'm right?"

"You had the best of intentions. Starting a unique business and doing some good, too. Setting out to help veterans find work. And that's exactly what you've done. Because sometimes, even with the best of intentions, plans don't work."

She was about to tell him that they couldn't know for sure this would work. If they didn't find enough clients and enough revenue, they'd fold in a year. And then her intentions wouldn't matter at all.

But his eyes were filled with a look of either pain or regret. She wasn't sure which and didn't want to press.

"It's good to know *someone* understands."

"More than just me. Julian, Ty, Michael. We all appreciate the work. I won't lie. I used to think the agency sounded like a charity. Then I wondered if this place was hiring out of a similar belief. And there's probably some of that. Wanting to help vets. I don't like it, but I get it now and I accept that it's a good thing. Some of us move around a lot. I've only been out for a while myself but I can't seem to find a job that sticks."

"Why?"

"It seems like I can never find anything that's hard enough. Challenging enough. Can't sit behind a desk, obviously."

"You do like to push yourself." She admired that about him, too. It was all she could do to haul her butt to the gym.

He gave her an easy grin causing her to think about last night and one other way in which he liked to push himself past limits.

"I like the way we're doing so well with our shared history. We're both very mature, I'd say."

"Agree."

"Neither one of us are even thinking about last night." That wasn't really true. She had thought about it, just not in the past few hours, though she was now of course. Hard not to.

"I'm not going to lie. Thought about it. At least twice today."

"Only twice?"

"Lied." He winced. "Twice an hour."

The pleasure those words elicited caused a shiver to skim down her spine and heat to pool between her thighs. He *didn't* regret them. The whole point of one more time had been to find out if it had been a fluke. She guessed neither one of them expected it to feel like the first time. To want more, and this time have an option. Except the option wasn't really there, or it shouldn't be.

She had to remember that.

"I thought about us, too, and I don't know what to do about that." Her voice sounded shaky.

"Let's forget last night happened."

Well damn, he seemed serious. *Forget* it happened? *Forget?* How was she supposed to do that when she hadn't forgotten in three years of his being out of sight and—mostly—out of mind? Apparently forgetting might be easier for this man than it would ever be for her.

She wouldn't let him know how much the words stung.

"Is that what you want?"

He stepped even closer and tugged on a lock of her hair. "No."

She was so relieved to hear the words, to see the slow smile on his lips, that for a moment she was at a loss for words. "Okay then."

He cursed under his breath. "Keep screwing this up. I'm trying to make this easier for you. To give you a graceful way to back out of what we started here."

"Do me a favor? Don't make things easier for me."

"Fair enough. I should ask you. What do you want?"

If she was being honest, and this just might be the time to do that, she would have to say that she wanted him. By her side. In her bed, or maybe his bed since her cot was now broken. Either way.

"All I know is I can't stop thinking about you."

Please. Don't let me be alone in that.

The pads of his calloused fingers tipped her chin to meet his gaze. "Do me a favor? Don't stop doing that."

"Sam," she whispered.

"Can't stop thinking about you, either, and you have to know I tried."

"So...tonight?" she asked hopefully. Jill batted her eyelashes. "Let's break your cot this time."

"I promised Julian I'd meet him and the men after work." He sighed. "And I'd break those plans in a second if it wouldn't be the fourth time I'd be breaking them. I'm trying, babe. It's exhausting but I'm trying to be social and not so much of a loner."

"You don't seem exhausted when you're with me."

"That's true. I'd say you're the exception. You always have been."

The words squeezed her heart and touched it in a way it had never been touched before. "That's possibly the nicest thing you've ever said to me."

"I would think you hear that all the time."

"Um, no. Try again."

He cocked his head. "What do you hear?"

"Can you tone it down a bit?"

"That I can believe."

"Sometimes my positivity seeps out into the conversations I have with others. It's all the affirmations I tell myself every day."

"Affirmations."

"Yeah, how else do you think I convince myself I'm a badass every day? You think this is just put together with luck and spit?" She widened her arms.

"God, you make me laugh."

But he wasn't laughing. His lips were twitching like he wanted to smile but there was no sound.

"You're not laughing, Sam." It had to be said.

"Oh yes I am, babe. Yes, I am."

With that, he walked away, but he did do it smiling.

Chapter Thirteen

That evening, Jill drove down the hill to her lonely little cottage on a small residential street in Fortune. An evening of Google searches on California indigenous wildflowers lay ahead of her, along with possibly a glass of wine or two. Or three. No doubt she'd do some thinking about Sam tonight, too. She'd start by remembering what it felt like to know she wasn't alone in her feelings. To know that he didn't want her to stop thinking about him. To understand he thought she was the exception. His exception. The smile that had twitched at the corners of his lips and the wicked gleam in his shimmering eyes.

Oh boy. She could fall hard for him.

Shakira waited in her trusty cage. After rummaging in the vegetable crisper for Shakira's steady diet of rabbit food, she carried a bowl to her cage and served Her Highness. Her little white ball of fur moved forward, pink nose twitching in anticipation, vacant eyes giving Jill nothing.

"Hello, Shak. How've you been, sweetie?"

Jill wasn't actually a rabbit person. According to Zoey, her kindred animal was a horse, but a bunny was the only kind of pet Zoey trusted Jill with at this point. She always deferred to Zoey in all things animal related. Zoey in turn deferred to Jill in all things fashion and makeup related.

Apparently rabbits liked quiet and calm and this often-empty house was perfect. Jill spent too much time away from home. Too much time working. The past two years had been like this, a nonstop cycle of work, sleep, work, and so it was no wonder that she hadn't met anyone. She hadn't even tried.

She'd been neglecting that side of her life, certain that she didn't need a man and without a doubt, didn't have any time for one. Opening one's heart meant being vulnerable and taking the only kind of risk Jill Davis didn't take. But now that she'd watched Carly settle into marital bliss with a baby and a hunk, all without sacrificing her career, Jill had hopes it could be done. And maybe she wanted that, too, someday.

In the meantime… Sam.

Was Wildfire Ridge still just a stop for him? Maybe after they got the park running smoothly and just when she would have come to depend on him, body, mind and heart he'd be on to the next big thing that challenged him. She wanted him to stick around for a while. There was an honor and goodness to him that she sensed and saw. Small parts broke through occasionally. A man who had a big heart and liked to help others. She'd seen a hint of that today.

He'd tried to encourage her when she'd needed a little pick-me-up. She'd had to be her own cheerleader for so many years that she'd almost forgotten what it was like to have someone be supportive instead of constantly worried.

He appreciated what she'd done, what she'd tried to do for veterans. Sam had said that good intentions didn't always match up with good results. He was only trying to be helpful but he'd aroused more questions about his past. Did Sam feel that he'd failed even with the best of intentions?

And who exactly had he failed? His fellow Marines? His parents? Did he carry pain or guilt over making his choice or was he really okay with never having anything more to do with them? The cold hard reality remained that this was probably something he'd never talk about. Because the odds were great that his was a war story, and she knew from personal experience that those stories weren't shared with people on the outside.

Even Ryan wouldn't talk to her. He simply found comfort in working with soldiers through Wounded Warriors and other organizations he supported. She was grateful he could talk to someone about what he'd been through. Everyone needed that. She hoped Sam had someone to talk to. But even if he did, she wondered if he'd take them up on it.

For now Jill had Shakira. Mostly. She took her bunny out of the cage and snuggled with her on the couch. But Shak wasn't much into snuggling. Her little nose twitched and she hopped off the couch, headed toward her favorite place in the house: under the kitchen table.

"You're not very social, are you?"

Jill really wanted a dog or a cat but when Shakira needed a home, she volunteered because she agreed she wasn't quite ready for the time commitment of a dog. Still, their eyes brimmed with intelligence as though they were almost human. Cats were independent and word out on the street was that they liked to snuggle. She could use a snuggle.

Jill poured a glass of wine and settled on her couch with her laptop. A stack of résumés sat on the corner of her coffee table. If she had already hired a general manager and split the load, maybe she could have assigned them this research and she could relax for a change. She could start to have a life again. No time for that now. Instead, tonight she would research California wildflowers. Size, shape and color, so that she'd be ready at the next council meeting. But as Shak sat under the table possibly planning her escape at daylight, Jill got pissy, wondering why Zoey didn't think Jill was ready for a dog.

Initially she'd thought Shakira would be the perfect pet. She was an adorable ball of soft fur and she'd been excited to give her a home. But Shakira didn't seem to notice the difference in whether Jill was home or not. Which might be the point of owning her according to Zoey. But surely after a year of being Shak's fur mommy she was ready to graduate to a pet that liked her, at least.

She picked up her cell. Zoey had barely said hello before Jill pounced. "Why do you think I shouldn't have a real pet, again?"

"Jill! She needed you." Zoey practically gasped. "Don't you *like* Shakira?"

"She doesn't like me."

"Of course she does. Bunnies just show their love in different ways."

"By hiding underneath my table? By never looking me in the eye? I think I'm ready for a dog. Or a cat. Or a small dog."

"Are you sure? Dogs are a huge responsibility. We're talking sometimes fourteen years of a relationship if you're lucky. And you're spending too much time away from home as it is. Spending the night in your trailer, I heard."

"Not anymore."

"Why? Finally get all caught up?"

She wondered if that would ever be true when it

seemed more obstacles were thrown her way every day. "That would be nice but no. My cot broke."

"How'd that happen?"

"Will my answer have any bearing on whether or not I'm qualified to be a dog mommy?"

"I don't think so."

"It may or may not have broken when Sam slept on top of me. Except that he wasn't really sleeping."

Zoey giggled. "Okay, so we've relaxed the boss/employee rule?"

"I don't know. Have we?"

"You tell me."

"Not really. It was just this once."

"Which was what you said about the first time."

"So maybe it was twice."

"Yes, I can count," Zoey said. "You realize what you're doing, don't you? You're doing that thing you do when you go after a guy who's totally unavailable. Which is why you're not ready to be a dog mommy."

"I can't have a dog because I pick unavailable men? That doesn't even make any sense. How about I *get* a dog because I pick unavailable men?"

"*And* you work too hard. Carly and I couldn't even get you to come out with us for a year when you were planning this park."

"This is a big deal. It means a lot to me. You know that."

"I do, which is why you haven't had the room for too many other big things in your life. Like a dog."

"Okay, okay. Listen, I know you're right about the pet. I'm not ready. Which is the only reason I haven't gone behind your back and adopted one anyway." She took a glance at Shak, now hopping back to her cage, leaving a trail of pellets in her wake.

Who preferred a cage to being allowed to roam free? Did she have a demented bunny or were all bunnies like this?

Zoey gasped, as if she couldn't believe Jill would go against her pet advice.

"Anyway, who says I'm not ready for a relationship with a nice guy? I am now. The problem is all I meet are unavailable men."

Like Sam. But he'd been so sweet to her today. He was trying. That said something. But it didn't say he was available.

"*Hmm.* Maybe you're attracted to men who are unavailable because *you're* the one who's unavailable. Oh, that's good. I'm going to write that one down."

But even if that had been true about her at one time, it wasn't any longer. Not since the moment she'd met Sam for the second time at the flagpole. And especially not since the night of the broken cot. He didn't seem to be as closed off as she'd initially thought. At least not with her. She was his exception. No doubt he was dealing with stuff so painful he couldn't talk about it. She had to give him that.

What he'd been through would remain private and all his until, and if, he would be willing to share it with her.

Intimacy was screwing with Sam's head again. He couldn't let it.

It wasn't like he hadn't gone without sex for very long stretches of time. During his deployments. During the long year of recovery in the rehabilitation unit in Germany. When the roadside bomb had exploded and hit the Humvee, it had thrown him about forty feet. He'd landed on his ass unable to feel his legs. But he'd done a hell of a lot better than Tim and Dave, who were gone. Obliterated.

Sam was the sole survivor, left behind so he could apparently feel sorry for himself for one interminable year. For a formerly active person, the sudden need for a wheelchair was nothing less than terrifying, even though the doctors told him he'd eventually regain use of his legs. Once he'd graduated to crutches, he began to see it would be possible. With an end in sight, he'd worked harder on his own recovery, picturing all the things he'd do again. Skiing. Riding. Hiking. Swimming. Things his friends would never get to do again. He'd always have some residual pain from a compressed spine, but he'd walk again. He'd hike and climb mountains and rocks. Have sex.

Somehow, because he was young, the doctors said, his body had healed well after the surgery and rehab. Not his mind. His mind was still in that dark and desolate place where he was to blame for everything. He'd failed to control the outcome. He hadn't saved his friends. Now he was back stateside with the almost-unbearable knowledge that his parents had been right. The thought was so ugly and raw that he resisted it. But it continually crept up and fought for space and top billing. Hikes helped. Keeping busy helped. He didn't want them to have been right. It meant he'd broken up a family for no good reason. It meant he'd broken far more than he could ever fix.

The look in Jill's eyes when he'd told her he couldn't stop thinking about her was both exciting and scary. She couldn't see he was doing her a favor by trying to stay away. He'd only affirm her insecurities and drag her down to his level of almost-constant darkness. It was selfish of him to keep seeking her out simply because she made him feel wanted and normal. He understood that was because of something she'd never know. In that hospital bed, and during rehab, for an entire year she was his happy place. She was the place his mind went to when the exercises were excruciating. The night he'd been with her was the last night he'd been normal in what turned out to be a long year of recovery.

Thankfully, he'd recovered from his incredible ability to say the wrong thing at the wrong time. He'd been able to admit not just to himself, but to her, that he didn't want to stay away. He couldn't get her out of his mind. He didn't know what to do with that in the head place where he was stuck, but if she wanted him he wouldn't be the one to deny her.

Other than Julian, who now ran with him every morning, Sam had tried to keep his distance from the men, who'd already formed some close friendships, he could see. Julian kept pressing and bringing him into the fold. But at thirty, Sam was the oldest in the group and he didn't like getting too attached if he could help it. Knowing that he'd feel too responsible if something went wrong. He could already see that some of them were too lax on the job. Ty and Michael certainly didn't push themselves though they had the ability to do so. But that was a relief to Sam for the most part, as he'd like everyone to stay safe. If there were any risks to take, he'd rather be the one to take them.

That meant he'd soon be taking a ten-mile hike over the entire ridge. Over dry and craggy terrain and off trails, he'd eventually suggest a two-day excursion with a stop or two for camping. Stargazing and that kind of thing. He planned to chart the hike using his own map. Maybe he'd actually meet up with one of the infamous mountain lions he'd heard so much about.

The next day, after completing the chores assigned to him, Sam headed back to his trailer late in the afternoon.

Jill stood talking to a firefighter he recognized as having been part of the friends and family trial run. The guy seemed to be into Jill, leaning in, laughing, shooting the shit like a champ. For her part, Jill tossed her hair and laughed, flirting with equal championship skill levels. The white-hot streak of jealousy that coursed through him split him in two. No idea why. He had no right to feel this way. No right at all.

"Sam," Jill said as he walked close enough to them to have to be acknowledged. "Remember Kevin?"

He shook the guy's hand. "Hey."

"How are you, Sam? That was a hell of a workout you put me through the other day. I'm still sore. But I had a blast."

"Then I've done my job."

"Kevin's just here to talk about the controlled burn they like to do up here—"

"Yeah," Sam interrupted and opened and shut his trailer door, effectively ending the conversation.

Rude, but he couldn't help it. He didn't feel chatty now. Or ever. Jill had company. Let her flirt with the handsome firefighter. He probably knew how to talk to women without insulting them. He might even be able to take care of himself and someone else, too. Sam was still working on that. Man, wasn't he a sad case? He was sick of himself.

After a few more minutes of flirtatious laughter and chatting he could hear drifting through the weak aluminum walls, Kevin left. Seconds later, Jill was at Sam's door.

"Can I come in?"

"Sure."

She hadn't been in here since the day she'd assigned him the trailer. Now she'd be able to see that he hadn't done a damn thing to make the place his own. No pictures up or signs of permanence. Somehow that was going to come back to bite him. She'd see that as a sign he had no intention of sticking around.

"What was that about just now? You just walked away when I was in the middle of a sentence."

"You were busy with your boyfriend. I thought you should get back to it. You're welcome."

"He's *not* my boyfriend."

Of course he knew that. Jill was not the kind of woman who hooked up with a guy when she was already with someone else. He shrugged, wondering if they'd let him back in grade school since he was acting like a child again. He'd fit right in, though the desk might be too small.

"Sam, what's going on? Things are weird between us again. This is exactly what I *didn't* want to happen."

She could join his club. He didn't want this, either. "If you want me to leave, I will."

"No, I don't want you to. Wait. Do you want to quit?"

He shook his head. For reasons he couldn't quite explain, he didn't want to go. Not yet. "I don't mind staying."

"Good. We'll work this out. If you want, we can be friends for now."

He scowled. "You want *me* as a friend."

"Why not? We have a lot in common."

"We do?" He racked his brain for what he might have in common with any woman, but especially one like Jill.

One who for reasons that weren't entirely her fault, had never pushed her physical limitations. One who highly respected the military and held it in the highest of regard. She had more in common with the old Sam. The Sam that went to war, and not the one that came back.

The man that came back was beginning to understand that his family had been right and his friends' sacrifices had been for nothing at all. Which meant that the past twelve years of his life had been wasted.

"For one thing, we both love Wildfire Ridge and want it to be successful. And you've been a friend to me. You helped me realize a few things. Maybe I did want to impress my family. But that's not the reason I did this. I want to help. I saw what Ryan went through when he got back home. He was one of the lucky ones. But I can't stand the fact that there's even one veteran in our country who can't find work. I know I can't solve the entire problem, but I have to do what I can."

Christ. That was it. The words hit him like a solid punch to the gut. She did pity him. All of them. This company was a charity of sorts. Her way of giving back, and while he might be able to take that from anyone else, he couldn't accept it coming from her. He wanted to kiss her pouty soft mouth and wring her neck at the same time. She was so sweet and pure and somehow untarnished by the world. Her intentions were so damned good. Perfect. She had no idea.

When it came to his service, she had nothing to thank him for at all.

He stepped into her, just got right up in her space like he didn't think he'd ever do again. "Sorry. I can't be your friend."

Her eyes widened in surprise. "Why not?"

"Because you piss me off sometimes."

"Oh."

He reached for her and wrapped one hand around the nape of her neck. "Also, I can't stop thinking about you naked."

She smiled. "I guess we have a problem, don't we?"

"And as problems go, it's a good one to have."

Chapter Fourteen

Good thing that Jill had finally agreed to go dancing at the Silver Saddle with Zoey and Carly, because between wildflowers and Sam, she had to stop overthinking.

Dancing was a much better idea.

Best of all, Zoey and Carly didn't want to talk about Sam or Wildfire Ridge's Outdoor Adventures. They'd christened tonight a work-free zone and a man-free zone. Not that Sam was Jill's man.

"Grace did the cutest thing yesterday," Carly said when they were taking a break.

"No!" Zoey held up her hand. "Baby-free zone!"

Carly made a face, then turned to Jill.

She raised her bottle. "Sorry, I have to agree."

"Then what do we talk about if we can't talk about work or men or our children?" Carly said.

"We...can talk about our pets," Zoey said tentatively.

"Falls too closely under work for you. To be fair," Jill said with a finger waggle.

They sat in silence for several minutes, enjoying the sounds of Thomas Rhett singing "Die a Happy Man." It was a slow, romantic song. A couples tune, and there were plenty of them on the dance floor. Some staring into each other's eyes like they were stupid with love. Others clung to each other. *Oh, sigh.* She wanted that, too. Wanted to be deeply in love for maybe the first time in her life. The real thing. He didn't have to be perfect. Just perfect for her.

The girls only danced to the fast songs with each other. Considering Carly was married, and Zoey and Jill wanted to dance and not hook up, it was a great arrangement. They occasionally had to explain this to a hopeful-looking man.

Jill slapped the table. "Okay! I want to talk about Sam."

She had expected them to protest, but she was wrong about that. Both Carly and Zoey turned to her, eyes wide and zoning in.

"Help me. I'm overthinking again," Jill said.

"You have a tendency to do that." Zoey nodded.

"Honey, knowing your family, you were trained to think in the womb," Carly said.

"But it isn't crazy, either," Zoey added. "To consider this thing between you and Sam carefully. You should."

"Right?" But when Jill thought back to one of the few times she'd acted purely on an impulse, she had to go back to San Francisco and Sam.

Generally speaking, she wasn't one to throw caution to the wind in either relationships or business. The night with Sam had been an anomaly. Now she found herself moving forward with him, and then pulling back. By all accounts he seemed to be doing the same. But her feelings for him had deepened after their second time together, and she hoped maybe his had, as well.

"You have to take a chance with him," Carly said. "You take some risks in business so maybe it's time to take a risk with a serious relationship."

Jill wanted that. She wanted to risk it all with Sam. But he blew hot and cold all the time. Earlier today, she could have sworn they'd made progress and she'd wanted to talk with him again before she left. But as she left to meet the girls, he'd barely looked at her. He'd been deep in conversation with Julian and she didn't want to interrupt.

Eventually, Jill, Carly and Zoey took to the dance floor hand in hand, getting jiggy with Garth Brooks's "Friends in Low Places."

After a few minutes, Jill hit the restroom and on her way out, caught Sam sitting in a corner by himself. Against the wall with no one behind him. Nursing a beer. Her heart squeezed because other than the uniform, the crew cut and the coin flipping between his fingers, he looked exactly like the night they'd first met. It hurt her heart to see him so alone. She headed his way, and he caught sight of her. She smiled but he didn't return it. Yep. Another step back. He stood, left a few bills under his bottle and walked out.

Oh hell no.

Jill wound her way through the dance floor, ducking couples and shrugging off Carly when she tried to pull her back on the dance floor. Sam Hunt, her second favorite Sam, sang "Leave the Night On." Jill loved this song. But *her* Sam wasn't getting away from her without saying hello.

"Hey!" she shouted into the night air.

He was next to his motorcycle, which he'd parked near

the front. Saddling up. He simply quirked a brow, as if to acknowledge that, yes, he'd *heard* her.

She impersonated a storm trooper as she stomped up next to him. "Are you leaving?"

"Too noisy in there."

"Well, it is a *bar*."

"Now it's too noisy out here." He put his helmet on. "Came in to get a drink. I'm done."

"Because you saw me?"

"No. I saw you and your friends when you came in."

"You've been sitting back there all this time and didn't even come over to say hello?" When he didn't answer, she continued. "Why do you keep doing this? Making it weird between us."

He straddled his motorcycle and started up the beast. It roared to life. And he ignored the question.

Jill had met up with plenty of obstacles in her life. Illness. Mean girls. Overprotective and disapproving parents. Failed business ventures. Screwed-up relationships. And now, a wildflower.

It wasn't easy to get her down for the count. Sam should know this about her.

"Let's go." She straddled his motorcycle on what little room was left right behind him. Just tucked in her dress on either side of her legs. Fortunately, she wore her cowgirl boots.

He twisted back and slid her the kind of scary look she thought he'd reserve only for someone who had kicked his Harley, not simply *sat* on it without first being asked.

"Jill, get off."

"No." She swallowed hard at the deep and no-nonsense tone in his voice.

He pointed to the bar. "Seriously, go back inside with your friends before I carry you in there."

She snorted. Let him try.

"Not until you tell me why you're being so mean." She wiggled, getting comfortable.

Sam gave her his back, shoulders appearing rigid under the black leather jacket. He may or may not have muttered a curse under his breath. Then he carefully and methodically removed his helmet and shut off the motorcycle.

"You're here with your girlfriends. Dancing with each other. I got the feeling it was a man-free zone."

"That's a cop-out. You've met Zoey. And that's Carly with us. They'd love seeing you."

"Sorry. I'm not the best company right now."

She thought back to the conversation she'd seen him having with Julian. "Did Julian say something to you? Does he…know about us?"

"No. I wouldn't do that to you. What we have is between us and no one else."

"And what do we have?"

She'd put him on the spot but she didn't care. One of them was going to have to come out and admit they had something special between them. Something worth fighting for.

And it would be nice if he went first.

When he didn't respond, she climbed off the motorcycle, using his back as leverage. She half walked, half strutted her way toward the bar.

"Good night, you pain in the neck." When she turned, he was right behind her.

It didn't take him but five seconds to have her pushed up against the wall of the building, two arms braced on either side of her. His eyes were hooded as he lowered one hand and oh-so-casually circled her neck.

"Pain in the neck, huh?"

His large body was tall and imposing as he towered over her. In his black leather jacket, biker boots and literally windblown hair, he looked wilder than usual. But her body hummed because she didn't feel at all threatened or trapped. Instead, another tingle rode up her leg and settled between her thighs.

"Actually the pain is lower but I was trying to be nice."

He grinned, slow and easy. "How low? Here?" One hand dropped from her neck to her butt and he squeezed.

Gulp. Oh boy. "Yes, you're in the general area."

His hand took a slow slide up her body, moving from her behind to the small of her back, her waist, along the curve of her elbow, and ending with her neck. He leaned in and kissed the pulse point there.

The pulse point reacted as if she'd swallowed a magic dancing bean. "Sam…"

His hands were busy, one now under her dress and easing its way to the elastic of her panties. She sucked in a breath at his touch.

"What?" he whispered into her ear. "You don't want this now?"

Her resistance, what little she'd thought she possessed, faded to black. She did want him, just not here in the back of the Silver Saddle and near the dumpster.

"Sure I do." To prove it, she wrapped hands around the nape of his neck. "Just maybe not…right here."

With his fingers, he tipped her chin and she met blue eyes that looked dark. He studied her from underneath long lashes. "Why not? Is it the dumpster?"

Among other things. They were outside, for one, and anyone could walk up and see them. She'd never had sex in public even if the idea was a little intriguing.

"Well, yeah."

"Funny. It would be perfect." He gave a sideways look

in its direction. "I did go through a lot of garbage in the desert and sometimes it still messes with my head. Maybe I don't like the idea of dragging you down with me." He took a step back. "I can make you happy for a little while, but maybe I'm never going to be what you need."

White-hot anger pulsed through her. "Who said I *need* anyone? I take care of myself, Sam Hawker. I know what you're trying to do here and it won't work."

He was trying to let her off easy, so she wouldn't feel guilty about having slept with him again. She heard his message loud and clear before he'd ever said one word.

He was still haunted by this past, which hurt her heart. But most disturbing of all was that Sam didn't feel good enough for her.

He quirked a brow as if waiting for her to elaborate.

"You want me to give up on you and I won't ever do that."

He cocked his head. "Anything is better than your pity."

They were going there again. To that place where he wouldn't let her feel an ounce of compassion for what he'd been through. She probably didn't know the half of it and never would, but whatever it was, he didn't deserve to carry this kind of pain around with him forever.

She drilled her finger into his chest. "For the last time, I don't pity you. I *hurt* for you. And you can't stop me."

The back door opened and out came Jimmy, the owner, carrying a trash bag. "Hey. Everything okay here?"

"Yeah," Jill said. "All fine."

Jimmy was former Army, and as he glanced casually in their direction, Jill noticed a two-second look pass between Sam and Jimmy. It was a simple nod in which a thousand words were exchanged between them. At *least*.

They didn't need words. She envied that instant tribal

connection that Sam had with Jimmy, with Ryan, with Julian and the other guys. It was the membership card to an exclusive club no one ever wanted to join.

Jimmy hauled the bag into the dumpster and strode back inside. For one second Jill heard the sounds of Brett Eldredge singing before the door muffled the sound.

"Go back inside with your friends," Sam said.

"Please?"

"Please, go inside." He strode back to the motorcycle and straddled it between long powerful legs.

She walked back to him before he could put on his helmet. Setting her hands on his shoulders, she met his indigo eyes straight on. Neither one of them blinked for one long moment.

She would try this "no words" gaze that had passed between Jimmy and Sam. That had often passed between Ryan and his war buddies. No, she was not former military and had only small clues of what they had been through. Ryan also didn't talk much about his service. But she had an imagination. A good one, last she'd checked.

And no matter what Sam had been through, no matter who he'd hurt or who he'd failed, that would never make her better than him.

She raised her hands from his shoulders to frame his face. Stared into beautiful blue eyes framed by long dark lashes. Then pressed her forehead to his.

"What are you doing?" Sam said. "The Vulcan mind meld?"

She pulled back in time to see his twitching lips.

"Shut up. I'm trying to tell you something."

"Words work, too."

"You're right." She traced the rough bristle on his jawline, thinking of the irony behind his words. "I'm not too good for you. I don't feel sorry for you. You keep telling me you're not what I need. Maybe that's true, but you're exactly what I want. And I reserve the right to make *that* choice for myself, Sam Hawker. You hear me?"

"Yeah," he said on a rough whisper. "I hear you."

He pulled her close and kissed her with a long and deep kiss that had her heart aching for an entirely different reason.

"Jill?" The doors to the Silver Saddle opened and Carly and Zoey stepped outside.

Jill slowly and reluctantly moved out of Sam's arms as they dropped to his side.

"Go inside, Mr. Spock. I'll see you later." He winked. "Get a good night's sleep because tomorrow I have a surprise for you."

She smiled and watched as he slipped his helmet back on, started up his Harley and drove away into the velvet dark night.

"What was that about?" Carly asked, coming to Jill's side.

Jill sighed. "That was just me, risking it all."

Chapter Fifteen

You're going to have to get your hands dirty sometime.

Jill floated in the cool waters of the lake, trying to get comfortable with the feel of a board strapped to her feet. Or strapped to the laced-up boots on her feet. The boots that matched the ski vest she wore over a pair of bright pink board shorts. She remembered ordering these from the catalog, thinking they would be a nice choice for their female clientele, not quite imagining she'd be the first to wear them.

Relax and fall forward.

Keep your arms straight.

Let the boat do the work of pulling you up.

Sam's next-day "surprise" had been to show up at her trailer shortly after she'd arrived to start her day, all the men in tow, to give her a wakeboarding lesson on the lake. They all seemed very excited about it, so she didn't have the heart to make excuses.

Surprise!

To his great credit, Sam *had* brought coffee with him. God, she adored this man.

Yes, it was time she tried another sport she'd never attempted before. The guys had been giving her a mini-lesson for the past thirty minutes. Soon it would be time to put it all into practice, if she could get all the parts moving and in sync. Since she'd never been accused of being graceful, either on the water or out of it, this could be a challenge.

But no, she was not afraid, worried, or intimidated. Nor would she back down. This was a job for her alter ego, Angelina.

That girl was a firecracker.

Julian was at the wheel of the boat a few feet away from her. Michael, Ty and Sam all provided instruction.

"Ready?" Sam said.

"Hell, yeah!" she shouted. Angelina did, anyway.

Sam went over the instructions once more and then smiled and gave a thumbs-up. She returned her slightly quivering thumb. Julian started up the boat and it began to slowly pull away.

Jill remembered to let the board drop, to let it slice through the water, relax her knees and… She forgot what was next. She managed to get up and stay up for three glorious seconds. Going under, she came up sputtering and blinking water from her lashes.

Sam and the boat were only a few feet away. "Once you're up, don't look down."

"What?" She shook her head, flinging water out of her ears.

"Keep your eyes on the boat—it will help with your balance," he shouted, pointing to his eyes.

"Okay," she shouted back, then gave him another thumbs-up.

Gosh, there was so much to remember.

"You can do this, bossy lady!" Michael called out.

"You know it," she said, not at all certain he was right.

The next few times weren't much better.

"Don't pull with your arms," Sam yelled over the loud whir of the motor. "Let the boat take you up."

"Okay."

She'd get up, a great achievement, but then couldn't stay up. And she was getting tired by the fifth or sixth time.

Sam dived into the water and swam to her. "You okay?"

"Sure I am." She didn't appreciate his furrowed brow. The obvious concern in his gaze. She gripped the baton. "Let's go again."

Moving closer, Sam's hand skimmed down her spine to her behind and he spoke softly. "You can give up now, babe. We'll try again another time. It was a good effort."

"No! I'm not done." She held the baton tighter. "How long did I stay up? Three seconds?"

"Five last time," he added helpfully.

"Really?" That was longer than she'd suspected since frankly she'd thought those three seconds had seemed more like one. "Okay, I think I can stay up this time for longer. I'm getting this."

Sam went over everything with her for the twentieth time.

"Last time," Sam said in no uncertain terms. "The guys want to break for lunch."

"Oh, of course."

This time, she was up, enjoying the spray of the lake's water on her cheeks, the bright summer sunshine nearly blinding her. And then she was down. Sam swore it was thirty seconds that time but she didn't believe him for one second.

And it wasn't until much later in the day that Jill realized that breaking for lunch might have been Sam's way of allowing her to stop without losing face.

Later that afternoon a dried Jill sat in her trailer, thinking about Sam's words on the day of their trial run. He obviously meant that for someone who'd opened an extreme sports park, she didn't seem all that interested in a good physical challenge. Now that he knew the reasons why she might be a little delayed in that area, he understood.

As she sat behind her desk, every muscle in her body ached in a good way. She'd forgotten how much energy swimming took out of her. She hoped today she'd shown Sam that she wouldn't give up easily. On anything or anyone.

Certainly not on him.

He kept quietly hammering away at her tired heart, putting it through the wringer.

She wasn't too good for him, and Sam of all people had a heads-up on one true fact about her. No matter what she looked like, and whether or not she resembled the girl-next-door type, Sam knew better. He should know she was far from perfect. She couldn't stay up on that board if her life depended on it. Yet.

She'd had plenty of limitations put on her. Even Ryan worried occasionally, though he was much better at keeping it from her. Sure, she'd never climb Mount Everest but she'd now been across the zip line at night. Holding Sam's hand, but she hadn't even needed him the second time. That was only the beginning of bigger and better things. Eventually, she'd rock climb and learn to stay up on a wakeboard and everything else, too. Climb a smaller mountain. Baby steps.

She checked email and found one from a board member who had suggested adding longer excursions to their offerings. One- or two-day trips to the mountains for rock climbing. Snow trips to the Sierras in the winter for skiing and snowshoeing. It would be another stream of income and a way to add interest. And she was again asked whether or not she'd had a chance to check out the résumés they'd sent over or interview someone for the general manager position.

But she would need more guides, not a corporate drone.

On it. Jill hit Send, and went back to her mountain of emails.

In her spare time, of which she had *so* much these days, she researched wildflowers. She'd been seeing them in her dreams. Pretty purple, blue and yellow flowers that grew tentacles long enough to wrap around Jill's neck and squeeze. The city council meeting was tonight and she'd be ready with a list of suggestions for how they could protect the endangered wildflower. Among them?

Put a little fence around the flowers with a marker describing their name and plight.

Hire a professional arborist to dig them up and move them to a different location.

And… Okay, she had nothing else. She needed more ideas.

Or maybe what she really needed was more of Sam. A little tension relief. More of his agile hands making his way under her dress and her panties.

But something else he'd said twice now bothered her. She'd done something very wrong if he thought for one second that she felt sorry for him. There was a difference between pity and compassion. She could never feel sorry for Sam, a man who'd lived his life on his own terms, made his choices and owned every one of them. He'd already accomplished what she'd tried so hard to do with her life. What she was still doing with this place. With her life. Moving forward, owning it, living on her own terms. Doing life, Jill's way.

Last night and again this morning she'd fallen a little bit deeper for Sam. She could continue to see him in secret. No one would be the wiser. But Sam wasn't anyone's dirty little secret and he sure wouldn't be hers.

Stretching, she forced herself to do fifty jumping jacks. Heart racing and fully functional thank you very much, she slowed down and felt a trickle of sweat roll down her back. Physical activity could be addictive. Sometimes she understood why Sam continually had to find the hardest and toughest physical challenge.

She stepped outside of her trailer into the warm day and blinked into the bright sun.

This afternoon the guides were busy coordinating routes and trails, and cleaning equipment after the friends' weekend. She took a walk down the trail toward the hill that stretched up a good two hundred feet and in the distance saw a mirage. It had to be one, because no one in their right mind would climb without a harness.

But yet there was Sam, freestyling it, while the men looked on from below.

For one brief moment she wondered if he was trying to sabotage this park. Or get fired. An accident could mean the termination of the park before it even opened. Cal/OSHA's guidelines for employees were strict and she had every intention of following them. Safety first. She didn't need her crazy adrenaline junkie employee/boyfriend pushing the limits. She wanted to yell but if she spooked him, he might slip off. Instead she quietly walked to the bottom, where Michael, Ty and Julian stood. Big smiles on their collective faces. Ty turned as he heard her walking toward them.

"What are we doing here?" Jill asked.

"Oh, um, hi, boss," Ty said, a frozen smile on his face. "Hey, good work today on the lake."

"You'll get it next time," Michael said.

"Uh-huh. What in the name of god is he doing?"

"Freestyling," Julian said, walking toward her.

"Oh, I'm aware of that," Jill said, trying not to bite off a piece of her tongue in fury. "The question of the day is why?"

"We may have bet Sam he couldn't do this," Michael said, looking as guilty as a sinner at church.

She already knew from experience it was best not to dare Sam in any way, shape or form. He'd dived into a cold lake and made her follow him. He'd broken her bed. What was next? Walking through fire? No. She wouldn't allow it. He would not do this to her or to himself.

"Are you mad at him?" Julian asked. "He's not going to get hurt. I would make sure of that. Seriously. He's done this before."

Mad didn't even begin to cover it. She was beginning to see everyone cross-eyed. That's how freaking *mad* she was.

She hooked a finger toward her trailer. "Tell him I need to see him immediately. My office."

The view from here was amazing. Not that Sam had much time for sightseeing. He was too preoccupied with not falling. With each handhold getting him closer to the top. Closer to proving to these bozos that it wasn't smart to dare him to do anything.

"Hey, Sam!" Julian shouted up to him. "Time to come down."

Ty whistled. "You're in trouble with the boss."

Great. He would have thought she'd be inside the trailer recuperating from this morning. Jesus, he'd practically had to pull her out of the water by her ear. The woman was fierce.

He sort of loved that about her.

But right about now she should be behind her mountain of paperwork on wildflowers. Speaking of which, he had to talk to her about that. He'd meant to give her the news after lunch, but then the men had dared him to freestyle.

It took him another few minutes to get back to where he could safely jump down the rest of the way.

He rubbed his hands together and threw a look at Julian. "Told you."

"Now go get your punishment," Michael said, leering. "Maybe if you're lucky she'll spank you."

"Nah." He scowled. "I do the spanking."

He left the men howling, though he didn't understand what was so funny. They all had a weird sense of humor in his opinion. Then again, maybe he simply needed to get one.

When he opened the door to Jill's trailer, she stood hands on hips, smoke practically coming out of her ears.

"You wanted me?"

"What the *hell* was that?" She pointed outside.

"I was freestyle climbing." He shrugged. "It's a thing."

"And why were you freestyling when we have plenty of harnesses and ropes for this?"

"A dare. And you never ask why someone would climb the face of a mountain. It's because it's there."

And sue him if he liked this Jill. A lot. When she

was fired up and as irate as she was at the moment, she couldn't waste her precious time feeling all this ridiculous *compassion* for him that he didn't want or deserve.

"You make me so mad." She slapped her desk.

His mouth was doing that weird tip at the side. "I can see that."

She stepped toward him and drilled a finger into his chest. "I want you to be honest with me. Are you *trying* to get hurt?"

He snorted. "Hell, no. I believe I told you the day you hired me—I'm hard to kill."

"That's not funny." She rested her palm against his chest. "Hard to kill but not hard to hurt."

His heart stiffened and tightened, as if anticipating a blow. She had become a weakness for him and could deliver a roundhouse kick to his second-favorite organ. He couldn't have that.

"Look, I know you can relate to taking some risks in life."

"Not ones like that."

"I always calculate the danger. But maybe everyone views taking chances in different ways." He removed her hand from his chest and threaded his fingers through hers. "You hired a bunch of adrenaline junkies. That's who your clients will be, too."

"That's true. But I need *you* to be guarded. I can't do this without your help."

Before "I need you" came out of her mouth, he stopped her. "You don't need me or anyone else."

As if considering it, she tilted her head and smiled up at him. "It's true that I'm a strong and powerful woman."

"Believe it. One who attacked my hand with an incredible bite."

"You asked for that."

"True. I brought you down into the gutter with me."

"Hardly. But I don't want to be worried about you when I'm busy trying to save this park from a wildflower."

"You won't have to save it from a wildflower. And you don't need to worry about me. Look, I'll tone it down. Honest. I'm not trying to get hurt." He brought up her hand to his lips and brushed a kiss across the knuckles because he couldn't help himself.

She took a deep breath. "Damn it, Sam. You really piss me off sometimes."

"Well, I excel at that. Sorry I scared you. I won't take chances like that again. At least not here."

His words were conciliatory while his gut churned. He wasn't ready for her. For any of this. But damn it all, he wanted to be. He wanted to be that man. More than ever.

"You drive me crazy but I love the way you drive me crazy." She stepped forward and let her head fall against his chest. "We don't have the best timing, do we?"

"And we meet in strange places. In a bar. On a flagpole."

"You're never going to let me forget that, are you?"

"Not a chance."

He wanted to kiss her again. Wanted to allow the warmth she gave him seep into every cell of his body. She made him feel all the things that he wanted to. Happy and useful. Calm. Not at all like there was a storm raging inside him that he had to suppress at all costs. With her, the storm could be controlled, but he couldn't allow her to be responsible for his happiness. It was too much to take on. Too much for anyone but especially for Jill, who didn't deserve the chaos he'd bring to her life. The ups and downs.

He both wanted her, but also wanted much better for her. Not sure where that left him.

"I'm not just worried about Cal/OSHA and our liability if you get hurt. You know that, right? I couldn't stand to see you injured."

"That's because you're the best boss in the world."

She didn't say a word but went narrowed eyes on him because yeah, he knew she was much more than his boss. She was more than he'd ever bargained for on one lonely night in San Francisco when they'd both taken care of each other.

"Come by my trailer before you go to your meeting."

"I don't think we have enough time——"

It was hard not to laugh. "Mind out of the gutter, babe. I did some research for you. On the wildflower issue. Found some environmental cases that might interest you."

She gaped at him. "Seriously?"

"Remember delegating? This time I did it for you. Next time? Ask."

She went from being pissed as hell at him to practically jumping into his arms and he realized he had buried his lead. He should have opened with the good news. Would he never learn?

"Thank you, thank you, thank you," she whispered into his neck.

"Babe, you don't have to thank me. You should know by now I'd do anything for you."

She smiled up at him, green eyes shimmering. "When I'm done with the meeting I'll come back here and let you know how it went."

"You do that." He kissed her forehead. "I'll be here."

He wanted to kiss a whole lot more but this was not the time. Instead, he simply traced the curve of her face one last time, stepped back and left her alone in her trailer.

Chapter Sixteen

Later, Sam wished Jill the best of luck at the council meeting where she'd fight for the right to coexist with a wildflower. Watched as her truck rolled down the hill on her way into town. He'd be holding down the fort. Later, when she got back, he would see what he could do about breaking his own cot. He was up for the challenge.

Unfortunately the comm system was on the fritz again when he left for his planned hike. It would have been nice to test the safety feature, but he packed his cell phone instead. It would do in a pinch, though he couldn't be certain what reception would be like the farther he went off trail. He had all the survival gear a man would need.

He checked in with the men before leaving, giving them a map of his direction. It wasn't the best time of the day to start a ten-mile hike, but he needed to get out of his trailer tonight. The walls were closing in on him. Suffocating him. And if he wound up spending the night under the stars, he'd be ready.

He set out before sunset, thinking about Jill. Thinking about the first time he'd ever laid eyes on her and how little he'd known about her. He'd imagined an entire life for her that came nothing close to the one she actually had. Turned out the real woman was a lot more complicated than the one that he'd spent several years pining away for. No wonder, since she was real. Complicated. And suddenly his pull to her wasn't easy and calm. Story of his life. But the thing of it was she was so much more than he'd pictured, too. Compassionate. She cared for her family, her brother and the disenfranchised. She worked so hard not to appear the slightest bit vulnerable, which made her three times as adorable. A memory rolled through of her, lying under him, her face rosy pink from exertion.

What a mess he'd made out of everything. Agreeing to work for her, even knowing that he'd have a difficult time keeping his hands to himself. Next, he hadn't stayed on the high ground, but wanted one more time just to see. Knowing deep inside that one more time would sink him for good. And so it had, because that's how he rolled. Never let it be said that Sam Hawker took the easy way out.

By sunset, he'd covered a good six miles according to his compass. Still not a single sight or sound of a mountain lion. He was beginning to think they'd moved.

The red sunset mixed with shades of blue would have been glorious had he cared about it. Instead, Sam took out his flashlight to light the rest of the way. He'd soon have to make a decision whether to spend the night out here or head back. Since he hadn't stopped thinking about shit he didn't want to think about, stuff that always seemed to come back to him after the sun came down, he kept walking. And walking. When the sounds of explosions and gunfire and the screams of his friends were fading into the background, he slowed down. He listened to the empty sounds of the night.

Wind. A rustle in or near the branches of a nearby tree. A mountain lion? He turned toward the sound, tripped and lost his balance. Though he tried like hell to regain his footing, Sam fell down a ravine straight into total darkness.

Jill had been sitting for close to an hour wearing her high-powered kick-ass pantsuit, and calmly waiting her turn to speak, when she took a good long look at the agenda. She wasn't on it!

During a fifteen-minute break, she nearly accosted Mark. "I thought you put me on the agenda tonight."

Mark wrinkled his brow. "For...?"

"Are you *kidding* me? A resident filed a complaint about an endangered wildflower on the ridge."

"Oh yes. She called the office yesterday and withdrew her complaint. It turns out she was wrong. Sorry about that." He walked past her on the way to the coffee dispenser.

"Sorry? You're sorry? Mark, you should have called me. I prepared for this! I researched California wildflowers of every type. Purple ones. Pink ones." She counted off on her fingers. "Sam helped. I have examples of how we could deal with the issue. I care about this issue. I searched the ridge. I... I..."

Mark held up a palm. "Wow. I'm sorry you went to so much trouble, but hey. This is *good* news."

"Yes. Yes, it is." She straightened her lapels and smoothed down her pantsuit. "And don't you forget it."

With one last look at Mark's confused face, she executed a flawless spin on her killer pumps and headed out the door. Carly had been right. Maybe Jill had a tendency to prepare for problems before they had even materialized. She figured it was a leftover from the years when she'd prepared for every one of her parents' objections before they could voice them. When she'd brought a permission slip home to attend a ski trip during her junior year, or prom night. They'd throw up every objection known to man and she'd knock them down like they were feathers and she was a hurricane. She didn't always win but let's just say she was brave in the attempt.

She really needed to learn how to relax and do some more of that delegating stuff.

Driving home, free at last from the confines of the council, she wanted to celebrate. But instead of cutting loose at the Silver Saddle like she used to do with the girls back in the day, she wanted a quiet celebration. Up on the ridge to the place that had somehow become her refuge. At first it had been a home away from home. The place where she spent her days and nights in a trailer planning. Dreaming.

As a result of her childhood, Jill had learned to stand back and watch others live a full life. Even years after strenuous physical activity was no longer an issue, she'd been stuck in the pattern. Sure, she'd played volleyball in college. She jogged occasionally and hit the gym, but when it came to most sports, she still admired from afar but never engaged. Until Sam had taken her out on the zip line at night, she hadn't realized how much she'd been missing. Too caught up in paperwork and planning, she'd almost been the last one to enjoy her vision come to life. But Sam had shown her that and so much more.

If she wanted to eventually enjoy this park, she would have to hire someone to help spread the workload around. Just as her board of investors had suggested. Letting go of a little bit of control wouldn't hurt at this point. It was time to stop working so hard and enjoy life for a while. Because that's what regular people did. Also, she had to stop all the affirmations and pretending she was this awesome fearless person and just *be* that woman.

She stopped home long enough to change and check in with Shakira—working on her ability to someday become a dog's mom—and then headed up the hill. Sam would like to hear the good news, no doubt. Her buddy. In the short time he'd been here he'd made himself invaluable. She couldn't do this without him anymore.

If he still held back from her, and she could see that in his deep blue eyes that held a pain and wisdom beyond his years, she could wait for his trust. He needed healing, and she had a feeling he would get it here. This beautiful place would do it for him. This land. This former hill of wildfires and wildflowers. Of ridges, a lake and rough terrain. Made for hearty people like Sam—and Jill.

Sam's trailer was dark but she knocked on it anyway. No answer.

"He went on that ten-mile night hike he's been talking about," Julian said from behind her.

Jill startled and turned to him. "What hike?"

"Thought he told you. He's had this great idea for an excursion hike. An overnight stay, you know, real good stuff," Julian said.

Ty walked up, hands in his pockets. "You're going to be able to charge a lot of money for something like that."

"Night hikes?" Why hadn't he told her that? Was he planning to spring it on her at the last minute? Another surprise?

She could barely keep up with him. Who hiked at night? As if they could read her thoughts, or more than likely her terrified expression, Julian added, "You definitely don't need to worry about him. He's got it covered."

"When is he coming back?"

"Don't know but probably sometime tonight. He left before sunset," Julian said.

Okay, okay. No need to panic. Because it was pushing ten o'clock didn't mean anything. He might even choose to spend the night out there on the farthest part of the ridge just to see if it would be feasible to bring a group out there. That made sense. Too bad he hadn't shared his thoughts with her.

"We were just going to go into town to the Silver Saddle," Ty said, and then waggled his eyebrows. "Want to come along, boss?"

"No thanks, guys. You go and have fun. I'll just hang out here and wait."

"Oh yeah, also the comm system isn't working again, but he took his phone," Julian said. "And he told us the way he was headed. Drew a map."

The communication system was still not working? She'd logged numerous calls into the company and on each visit they'd fixed it only for it to go down again. Another issue to deal with.

"Which way was he headed?" Jill asked.

Julian came back with a roughly drawn map in Sam's handwriting. "Should we stay with you?"

"No, it's fine. I'm sure, like you said, he'll be back later tonight."

The men took off, Michael running to hop in the truck at the last minute.

It was good that Sam had drawn a map of his direction. Smart. He'd taken his phone with him, also smart. Problem was, it probably didn't work too well that far out on the ridge. Hence the need for a comm system. She tried dialing him anyway and got no answer. Of course, that didn't mean he was out of reception. Maybe he'd turned the phone off to save the battery. Or maybe he'd lost his phone when a mountain lion attacked him and ate his phone. Now he could be lying in a pool of blood. A big cat circling him, waiting to move in for the final kill.

She needed to get a grip.

He could handle himself. Jill realized that. But she couldn't stop thinking that she wanted, needed, to see that he was okay. She had a map of the direction he'd set out. Thanks to Sam, she was keyed up and ready for adventure. He'd said she was brave. Well, maybe tonight she would prove it to herself. She gathered supplies though she realized Sam would have taken everything he needed. Except a way to communicate. Not entirely his fault, but damn him.

After she'd changed out of her pumps and power suit, she stuffed a backpack with water, flashlights, matches, gloves and a first aid kit, then she took a deep breath and phoned Ryan. She forced some false calm into her voice. "Hey, you. How's it going?"

"What happened?"

Leave it to Ryan to read her emotions even across the cell towers. "Nothing much. I'm just going for a little night hike and if I don't call you back in…say three hours, then send a search party. 'K?"

"Are you out of your mind? Why are you going on a night hike? When's the last time you went on a hike of any kind?"

Don't remind her. She hadn't exactly been little miss athlete growing up and Ryan knew it well. Still, she'd been active for years and she was going to own this hike.

"I'll have you know I hit the gym four times a week. Okay, two."

"What's this about?"

"One of my employees set off on a night hike and he isn't back. I'm…worried."

"Let me guess. Sam."

"Yes. He means well. He's got this great idea and he's just trying to scope it out first."

"Don't go anywhere. I'm on my way."

"I'm okay. Trust me. I've got this!"

"Jill, no—"

She ended the call. Big brothers had a knack for being overprotective, and given her history that might be expected but Ryan was simply overreacting. It kind of ran in the family. Sam was right that she would have to get her hands dirty eventually. Today was the day.

She would be a part of this park and the extreme sports set if it killed her, which it just might.

Never much of a runner, Jill started off at a slow pace. Endurance was more important than speed, or at least that's what she'd told herself as a teenager when she couldn't run a mile in under twenty minutes. Her classmates laughed and asked whether she could also walk that fast.

The first rustling sound in the trees had her picking up her pace. Mountain lions and coyotes lived on Wildfire Ridge. Occasionally they even came down to the adjacent neighborhoods and homes around the base of the hill, but this was their territory. And she was the trespasser.

When the sun made its final crest over the slope, she pulled her trusty flashlight out. Swallowed the pebble in her throat and lit the way ahead. Better to see danger ahead than be ambushed, right? So even though she half feared she'd see a pair of amber eyes belonging to a mountain lion glowing behind a shrub as she approached, she let the light shine like a beacon. And just in case Sam was lying somewhere bloody from an attack, she'd want him to know someone had come.

She started calling out his name every few minutes, hoping there was no one else out here that went by the name of Sam.

Sam didn't know where he was. There'd been an explosion and now he was alone. Tim and Dave were gone. Sam had been driving. Must have hit an IED. He tried to remember more and couldn't. He patted his gloved hands down the length of his body. No blood. No missing pieces. But he panicked when he couldn't move his legs. He was numb. God, no. Sweat poured off him in the blazing heat of the desert. No...no...no.

He shook it off. No. He wasn't on the side of the road having been thrown from a Humvee. His leg hurt but the point was that he *felt* something. And man, it was so much better to feel pain than to feel nothing. To be numb.

He was going to be okay.

When he'd taken a header, he'd managed to reinjure his right leg; the one that had taken most of the work to repair in PT.

Two hours in this ditch and Sam finally heard the mewling sound of a big cat crying out in the night.

"Now? Now you choose to show yourself?" He pulled out his Buck knife from the sheath strapped to his good leg and spoke through gritted teeth. "Come on over here, sucker, because I'm in a bad mood and I could use some company."

His cell phone worked only to give him the time so he could know how long he'd been stuck here, his bad leg injured from having slipped down the ravine. Naturally, he couldn't get a signal. He'd stretched as far as he could in every direction and held it over his head. No go.

As the temperatures continued to fall, Sam accepted facts. He was stuck here all night. In the morning, when he'd have light and a better view, he would make a splint for his leg and crawl up the ravine. Maybe he'd get a better signal or maybe he'd walk with a hitch in his step all the way back. Either way. He reached into his bag and, flashlight between his teeth, found the collapsible tent and set it up near the rock he'd almost landed on. It would at least keep him warm if not comfortable.

"Sam! Sam!"

He heard Jill's voice, so now he was hallucinating. Then the sound of the big cat again. Perfect nightmare scenario. Jill and the mountain lion. Someone he'd die to protect and his ability to protect had been decimated. He hadn't had a waking nightmare in a while and thought he was past all that.

"Oh god. Was that a l-lion? H-hello? S-Sam? This isn't f-funny."

When the flashlight hit the tree branches above him, he realized this was no waking nightmare. It was Jill and she sounded out of breath. She'd hiked six miles out here?

"Jill? What the hell?"

"Sam!" Her flashlight followed his voice down the ravine. He flashed his into her wide eyes as they blinked and took him in. "Oh god. You're hurt."

"I'm fine."

Fine was probably overkill but he wasn't in the business of worrying people, least of all her. He'd just promised her he'd tone it down and now look at him. This wasn't supposed to happen. He was supposed to help people. Save them. It was extremely humbling to be in this weak position in front of the last woman he wanted to see him this way.

"You shouldn't have come. Where are the guys?"

"They went into town because, unlike me, they thought you'd be all right. Figured you could handle anything that happened."

"Well, they were right. You can go back. I'll see you in the morning."

"No way. I am not leaving you, Sam Hawker! You're high if you think that."

"Not high, but I wish I was." He groaned a little and bit it back.

"What did you hurt?"

"My leg. Probably just sprained badly. I need to make a splint for it and then I can hobble back. It might take me a little longer."

"Really? It might take you a *little* longer, will it?" She snorted. "Hang on. I'm here to save you. Sit back and take it like a man."

"I don't need saving. I just need a good solid straight branch."

"I'm coming down." She swung one leg down the ravine, cresting the giant root of a tree.

"Stay up there. I mean it."

The big cat mewled again and for the life of him sounded much closer.

"Jill, get down here. Now."

But he hadn't needed to tell her because Jill heard the cat, too, and she pretty much skied down the ravine on her butt cheeks.

"Mmph." Her momentum pushed her forward and she landed with her face practically in his crotch. "Oh, hi," she said to his dick.

He shone the flashlight in her face so she could better see whom she was greeting. It was difficult not to laugh even in this humiliating situation. One look at her wide eyes when she realized whom she'd said hello to and he really did laugh.

She straightened and started waving her hands above

her. "That lion sounds hungry. We're in his territory. Don't forget to appear larger than you are."

"You go ahead and do that. I've got a weapon." He patted his Buck knife.

"You won't have to kill it. Ryan should be right behind me—I'd say about twenty minutes or so. Maybe sooner because he's faster than I am. I called him and told him to send a search party if he didn't hear from me. I doubt he listened. I'm sure he drove up here right after I hung up on him. You drew a great map."

"I only drew one map."

"Yeah, and I took a photo of it with my phone and left the other one taped to my trailer door."

"Smart."

To recap. This girl could handle her scotch, didn't give up easily, had the guts to follow him out here alone at night, the intelligence to first call for help, leave a map and, oh yeah, she was gorgeous and kissed him like she wanted to inhale him.

Why did he have to meet the best woman for him at the worst time in his life?

That would be because if not for bad luck he'd have no luck at all.

"Don't worry, they'll be here soon."

"I'm not worried."

"No, of course not. For that, you might have to accept that you need help."

Those words hit him like a sledgehammer to the heart. He needed help, but not from her.

"What happened to your leg?" She touched lightly, rubbing from his thigh to ankle, eliciting a different kind of ache altogether.

He leaned his head back, resting it on a rock. "I probably reinjured it."

"Reinjured?"

"It was first injured in Iraq." He closed his eyes. "But it wasn't a big deal. The bigger deal was my compressed spine and the fact that I couldn't walk for a while."

"Couldn't walk?"

He figured he might as well scare her off now and permanently. These uncomfortable feelings, the pinch in his chest to realize she'd come after him because she was worried—this was all stuff he didn't need or want. It was one thing to be physically drawn to her but another to feel close. Intimate. As if she understood *who* he was. She didn't know who he was, but maybe she should.

"Roadside bomb. It threw me forty feet but my injuries were mostly internal. Compressed spine. I had surgery but there's still some residual pain. I'll probably be a cripple by the time I'm fifty, but I was lucky."

Tim and Dave not so much, but Sam wasn't going to talk about them. Ever.

"Oh, Sam. I'm sorry." She rested her head against his chest. "That must have been so hard."

He felt her pity, wafting through the scent of the night, thick as a forest. The last thing he wanted. "I thought I told you. *Don't* feel sorry for me."

"I'm not feeling sorry for you," she protested. "It's simply compassion. Empathy."

"Or pity."

"Not *pity*. Remember, I know what it's like to be pitied. I also know what it's like to be physically stuck for a while. But I still can't imagine what you went through in that desert so far away from home."

"Sounds like pity to me. Look, I walked into the service of my own free will. Feel sorry for someone else. For the people who live there and have no choice. I had a choice."

"Can't I do both? I admire you for your courage. For trying to help."

"And for failing? Do you admire that, too?"

"It's not about failing."

"War is always about winners and losers." He winced, the nerves in his ankle shooting radiating pain through his leg. "There's no in-between."

She didn't speak for several minutes, during which time he took the opportunity to listen for the cat. Or for the sounds of people arriving. The crunch of boots on twigs and branches. Their voices in the distance. He heard nothing but the sound of her breathing. They were in this pit alone and she was so close he could smell her hair, a flowery scent that reeled him in every time.

"How long was it before you could feel your legs again?" Her voice was muffled as she spoke into his chest.

But he heard her loud and clear. "About a year."

She sucked in an obvious breath and every muscle in his body tightened.

"Watch it," he warned.

"I just didn't know."

"If I seem like I take chances and I'm on the move a lot, it's because I know what it's like not to be able to move. Again, I told you. I'm lucky."

"You don't sound so lucky some days."

"So I'm not Mr. Personality."

"Actually, you're fine with me most of the time. Zoey thinks you're great. I just think you could have been nicer to Hunter."

"Why? Should I lie to him or tell him the truth? Which do you think he'd rather hear?"

"Why would you lie to him?"

"Never mind."

There was no point in discussing this. Not with a civilian. No point in explaining that war wasn't like it was portrayed on TV or in the movies. War was grown men screaming like little boys. Grown men crying for their mothers. *That* was war.

"Is it regret? Is that what you're feeling?"

"That's a beginning."

He didn't know why his tongue was so damn loose tonight. Sure didn't have to tell her every small thing about his life so she'd know who she was dealing with. But the night was quiet now. She was soft in his arms, her hair tickling his nose. Memories came back to him of how he'd initially struggled in PT because he had no possible end in sight. Once they'd given him his medical discharge papers, nothing remained. He was done. Nothing left to work toward. Nothing except the memory of that night. Of her. She meant *normal* to him. She was like a red beacon shining in the distance telling him one day he might feel whole again.

"Was your family told about the accident?"

Accident. Is that what she called it? An accident was unexpected. Unplanned. One could argue he should have expected this. He'd been in a war zone, after all.

"No choice. The US government didn't ask my permission but simply contacted next of kin. However, they couldn't make me see them. And I didn't."

"Sam—"

"Did I mention I got some of the best medical treatment in the world?"

"But you needed someone *there* for you."

I did have someone there for me. Someone I'd met only once. You're never going to know about that, either.

"I didn't need two people there who would say 'I told you so.' And then I'd have to admit to myself something

I've never wanted to admit out loud." He hitched in a painful breath. "They were right."

She raised her head from where it had been lying on his chest to meet his eyes. He caught sight of the fire in green eyes lit only by the glow of the full moon.

"They weren't right. You were right to follow your conscience. And they were wrong not to support their son, even if they disagreed."

"It's not that simple. They stuck to their beliefs even if it meant giving up their only child. You have to admire that about them."

"Both you and your parents sound incredibly stubborn. What about love, Sam?"

"What about it?"

"When you love someone, you have to take the good with the bad. We're all just doing the best we can. But if we don't love each other, what do we have?"

"You have people who are related to each other but don't talk to each other."

"And you have an employee who doesn't have an emergency contact."

"Exactly."

"Now I know everything I need to know about you. Everything that matters, anyway."

"And you better run. Fast. Because I don't know how much longer I can keep away from you. I'm trying."

"Sam—"

He heard voices calling out in the distance.

"Jill!"

"Sam!"

"Our rescue crew has arrived," Sam said, squeezing Jill's hand.

Jill stood. "Guys! Over here."

Chapter Seventeen

Even though there was at least one mountain lion some-where around here possibly circling them and hoping for a snack, Jill was a little sorry to see this side adventure come to an end. Ryan arrived with Michael, Ty and Julian in tow. The four guys perfectly executed Sam's rescue plan. Sam instructed them the entire time, encouraging them and praising them for following instructions to the letter.

Good grief. He had to be a leader even now. Strong even when injured. He slayed her.

Tonight, he'd broken her heart bit by tender bit. He was so much more than she'd ever imagined. Broken, just as she'd once suspected. Beautifully broken. And Zoey got to be right again. Sam really was the wolf licking his injured paw in a corner. Unable to let anyone touch or help him. At least, not for what was aching inside.

"Should we get some medical attention for that leg?" Ryan now asked.

"I'll be fine," Sam said as he favored his left leg and hopped up the short steps into his trailer. "Think I just sprained it."

"Nice try, but you need to get checked out," Ryan called out, then pointed to Jill. "You."

"Don't start with me."

"I asked you to wait for me."

"Sorry."

But if she hadn't, she wouldn't have been in that quiet place with Sam where he'd told her more than she'd ever thought he would. More than Ryan had ever shared.

"Yeah, yeah." Ryan shook his head. "I'm glad you were with him until we got there. It's…a tough place for a soldier to be alone. Might have brought back memories."

She hadn't thought of that, and her heart filled as she wondered if that was why Sam had talked to her. Maybe she'd helped push some of the worst memories away.

"I was glad to be of help to someone."

"You're a help to all of us." Ryan ruffled her hair as if she was eight years old.

"Thanks, Ry-Ry," she said, in a valiant effort to make him feel ten again.

"You're taking him to the hospital."

That wasn't a question. "Yes, I will take care of it."

"Do it no matter what he says." He waved and was off.

Once the guys were all finished telling Sam what a rock star he was, Jill had him alone in his trailer. He lay back on his cot, one arm flung over his face, his leg elevated. Looking none the worse for wear. He was so gorgeous and strong even now. Intense blue eyes that cut her to the quick. No surprise she'd risked so much for one night with a stranger. With this man.

I don't know how much longer I can keep from falling for him.

"What?" he asked as if he wondered why she was still here.

"Do you have ice?" She went to the small fridge and searched the freezer. Found ice, wrapped it in a dish towel and brought it to him.

Studying her carefully as if he had to weigh her every move, he watched from lowered lashes as she sought to put the ice where it might do the best work. She ran it from his thigh to his knee and down to his ankle.

"Where does it hurt, exactly?"

"A little higher."

She moved from his ankle to his shin.

"Higher."

She moved the ice to his knee.

"Higher."

"Is it your thigh?" She moved to his muscular thigh, silently wishing he'd injured his steely buttock instead.

"No, just a little higher. You're almost there." He smirked. "And move to the middle."

She smiled, finally onto him. "I thought it was your leg."

"You can't blame a guy for trying."

No, she couldn't. Especially when the guy was sex on a stick. She wanted badly to indulge him but other matters took precedence.

"I'm taking you to the hospital. To get checked out."

"I'm fine."

"You would say that if your leg had been cut off. You're going!" She went hands on hips.

He grinned, slow and devastatingly sexy. "Kinda like it when you get bossy, got to admit."

"Well, they don't call me 'bossy lady' for nothing."

A few minutes later they were inside the curtained bay of the local hospital's emergency room. Sam was on a hospital cot, arms folded behind his head looking like he would kill someone with his bare hands. The X-rays had come back and the doctor had delivered his verdict.

"I don't know why you're so mad," Jill said. "We can find other stuff for you to do on opening day."

Since their grand opening was in one week, Sam would be unable to participate in the guided tours and events. There was a hairline fracture in his ankle from an old injury, and given his history, the doctor recommended a surgical boot to be worn for six weeks. The look on Sam's face when he heard the news told Jill that the doctor might as well have said "a year." Or "forever."

He continued to stare at the ceiling. She worried that he'd been taken back to the time when he couldn't walk and it probably wouldn't do her any good to argue that this wasn't the same at all. But given his reluctance to enter the hospital once they'd arrived, and him developing a thousand-yard stare at the bright lights and sterile smells, she had a feeling he was stuck. Stuck in that terrible place in the desert alone. Likely filled with regret and conflict all in the past but warring now in his memories. She'd followed close behind him to triage, but wouldn't have been allowed to go with him until Sam gave the okay.

"Sam?" She touched his elbow. "Are you okay?"

It surprised her when he jerked at the touch, then turned his head to her and slowly smiled as if seeing her for the first time. He reached for her hand, threading his warm fingers with hers.

"I'm okay, Boots."

"Because it's just six weeks." She squeezed his hand. "It will go fast."

It hadn't escaped her that he hadn't pushed her away tonight. Maybe he finally understood their relationship was such that she cared deeply about him. The thought of him being seriously injured on her watch...this was *Sam*.

"Sure. Time will fly with you riding my ass and making sure I don't further hurt my leg."

"Did you say riding you? Because I can do that." She moved from the chair she'd been sitting on and squeezed her body next to his on the cot. "Move over."

"Ow."

"Oh god, I've hurt you." She made an attempt to climb off, but his two arms restrained her, pinning her in place.

"Relax. How else am I going to get you to kiss and make it better?" He pressed his lips to her temple. "And you should know, if I'm really in pain I won't use the word *ow*. I have an arsenal of curses I'd use instead."

She smiled and met his warm lips, feeling the same old kick start to her heart whenever Sam was this close. That feeling didn't seem likely to fade anytime soon.

God, she loved him so hard and that was terrifying.

"Okaaay, you two lovebirds," the nurse said as she opened the curtains. "Sorry to interrupt but it's time for some actual medicine now, not just the kind that puts stars in your eyes."

Jill scrambled off the cot and waited in the lobby while Sam was fitted with the boot. By the time they got back to Wildfire Ridge, it was nearly two in the morning. Sam had no trouble walking up the steps to his trailer, and she followed him inside just to make sure he had everything he needed. No other reason.

"Can I get you something?"

She followed him to his cot, where he took a seat.

"About that ride."

He wanted her even now. Such a guy. Then again, speaking for herself, she wanted him even more since he'd shown a vulnerable side of himself. She'd fallen even deeper tonight. Still, she didn't want to be responsible for any further injury.

She sat next to him. "But your leg."

"I won't use my leg." He grinned and slid his thumb across her lower lip.

"I'd like to see that." Sam wasn't exactly a passive lover.

"So would I. You, riding me like a bronco? It's my favorite view on earth."

She wanted him more than her coffee every morning, but first he had to know a few things. Because everything had changed for her since the night he'd broken her cot. Now she wanted him to know how much he'd changed her life for the better without even trying.

"I have something to tell you." She straddled him and unbuttoned her top, wasting no time slipping it off her shoulders.

"Okay, I stopped listening. Might want to put that top back on." His teeth pulled in his lower lip.

Her black satin push-up bra at work. She smiled and shrugged back into her blouse. Then she trailed her fingers down his rock-hard abs eliciting a groan out of him.

"You have to know something. I never stopped thinking about you after that first night. Actually, the Chris Scale was revised because of you."

He narrowed his eyes. "The *Chris* Scale?"

"It's a complicated rating…but that's not important right now. The point is I thought I'd run into a gorgeous man who was extremely good in bed and not much more than that. And I tried to tell myself that over the years even as I compared everyone else to you."

"Babe." His voice was low, rough.

"But I didn't know who you were inside. I didn't know that you're smart and strong and loyal. And I feel so lucky that I ran into my one-night stand even if it was while I was stuck on a flagpole."

"Yeah, that was funny. I'm not going to lie."

She smiled and bent to kiss his pec. "Can I take my top off now?"

"Don't make me beg."

She removed her top slowly this time, slipping it off one shoulder at a time and enjoying every moment of watching as the light in his eyes deepened to the dark blue of the bay. They heated further as she tossed the blouse to the side and unsnapped her bra. She was gratified when he licked his lips.

She rose to divest herself of her cargo pants and matching black panties. Then she did the same for him before she straddled him again with nothing between them but air.

"You're so beautiful," Sam said almost reverently, his hand around the nape of her neck and lowering her to him.

He kissed each breast tenderly, then sensuously licked a nipple with his warm tongue. When he drew each nipple in and sucked, heat consumed her, tightening her belly. Tightening everything. She pulled him even closer, feeling him grow instantly hard between her legs.

"Why are you so irresistible to me?" he roughly hissed into her hair.

"Just lucky."

At the moment she was the luckiest woman alive to have met this man, not once but twice in her life. This time maybe at the right time. He'd opened up to her tonight, hadn't he? In a big way, he'd made himself available. He'd unlocked the door. Now it was up to her to walk in. To risk her heart for once and not just her body.

It was like winning the lottery twice. He was all the

things she'd ever wanted in a man wrapped up in one gorgeous hard package. Strong but vulnerable. Courageous. A beautiful warrior. Beneath his tough exterior was a man who'd been hurt in a much deeper way than she'd imagined. She had a feeling that she didn't know all of his pain, either, but he'd given her enough for now. Some hurts were too tough to talk about. She understood.

She pulled back and licked from his neck down his pecs to his abs. Taking him in her hands, she stroked him, enjoying the way his entire body tensed and he gave himself over to her. Letting her take control. He handed her a condom, which meant he'd definitely been planning or hoping for more of this, too. Encouraging. She protected them both then sank on his erection as he gripped her hips tightly.

Sam thrust into her, unable to hold back. She clung to his shoulders, riding both him and the crest of the wave. When the sweet pressure built she finally burst into a million tiny pieces.

Afterward, she lay spent in his arms. Her fingers trailed from his wide shoulders down to his strong biceps.

"What are we going to do about this?"

"This?" He nuzzled her neck.

"*This*. You and me. I don't want to stop."

"Never." He drew her close, his arms tightening around her.

She hadn't ever expected that Sam would be the right man. He'd simply been a hookup. And she wanted someone who would be open to a relationship. Someone whole. Now she could see that Sam had been broken in all the right ways. He'd put himself back together through sheer determination and will and she admired that about him. He was still a work in progress—then again so was she.

But in the process of getting to know him, in the pursuit of hooking up, she'd let her heart get involved. She'd fallen for him. *Hard.*

And she didn't have any idea what to do about that because now there was no turning back.

Sam woke with a start. For a moment he didn't know where he was, but then soft hair that smelled like flowers tickled his nose and he remembered. He was on Wildfire Ridge and had a soft woman in his arms. *Jill.* This woman, who was now far more than a simple memory he brought out when he needed to remember a better time. She was real and in his arms. *His.* This felt far too good.

He wanted to believe he wouldn't ruin this. That he wouldn't somehow say the wrong thing. Something stupid or hurtful or both. He wanted to believe he wouldn't somehow push her away. This was another chance, and one he didn't deserve. He understood the way she saw him and wanted to be that man. She was beautiful and kind and loyal and far too good for a jarhead like him. But because she believed in him, he had started to believe in himself again. He hadn't been responsible for everything that had gone wrong in the arid desert. Even if he'd switched seats with Dave. If not for that, maybe Dave would have been the one thrown. There was no way to know for certain. He was going to let that go.

Judging by the hint of sunlight he saw through the window blinds, it would be morning soon and she'd spent the night with him. While he didn't want her going anywhere, he was certain she didn't want to be found coming out of his trailer by any of the other employees. Their relationship, such as it was, had to be secret for now.

"Jill." He nudged her. "Boots."

"Mmm," she said, and nestled in closer.

"Want to wake up?"

"No."

"It's morning."

"Okay."

"The guys all get up early and usually Julian drops by for a run."

She jerked awake and sat up ramrod straight. "Oh."

"Yeah."

"I probably shouldn't be here." She rolled off the cot. "They'll want to check in with you. See how you're doing."

"Which is great. I'm doing great."

She picked up clothes off the floor and started shoving them on. "Really? You're already good?"

"Well, I had some pretty good medicine last night."

She jutted her hip out and gave him a look. "*Pretty good?*"

"Fantastic."

"That's better." Fully dressed now, she leaned to give him a kiss.

He pulled her on top of him and made it last. And last. When he had her panting and breathless, he figured it was a good time for her to go. This way she'd want to come back.

"I'll see you later." She stood again. "I'll be in my trailer drinking all of the coffee. All of it."

Hand on the doorknob, she turned back to him. "You're taking it easy today. Agreed?"

"Sure, boss, but I'm not going to just lie here all day."

She scrunched up her nose like she was considering it. "Maybe you can supervise. Actually, I could use your help in the office, too."

He quirked a brow. "In the middle of the day? Is that wise?"

"Not *that* kind of help! I actually meant…real help. On the financial prospectus for the investors. The numbers."

Sam yawned. "Sorry, did you say something?"

"I know it's boring but numbers don't crunch themselves."

"A sad but true fact."

She waved him off and was out the door. Thirty minutes later, there was a knock on the trailer door. Had to be Julian. He'd been coming by lately to join him for a run. Sam was no idiot. Julian had been slowly breaking down walls. He'd ask simple questions and eventually Sam talked. Not about that medal, not about Tim and Dave, but about where he'd been and some of the things he'd never un-see. He found it helped talking to someone who didn't blink an eye because they'd been there, too.

But Sam opened the door to Hunter, the kid. "Hey. What's up?"

"I came here with my Mom's friend Hudson. He's checking with Jill about a controlled burn they're going to do here later this month. Brought you some coffee." The kid handed over a foam cup. He stood in that awkward gangly way only a lanky teenager nearing six feet tall could pull off.

"Thanks. Come in." He nodded to the small living area near the kitchen.

It was odd the kid had sought him out, and he had to give him props for nerve. He hadn't been the friendliest person.

The kid was probably here for round two. His high and tight haircut was already in place. He was so ready to prove himself to the world. Caught up in his angsty teenage self. His invisible teenage self. Sam had been that indestructible teenager. The one who was so certain he was right that he wouldn't entertain any other possibility. He almost missed the kid he'd been. Life had been so simple then. Orderly. He'd had it all mapped out. A plan that couldn't fail. But if he'd only listened to someone, sought counsel from someone older, would his life have been any different or would he have found other ways to screw up? One thing he did know. This kid would have to find out for himself and no one would stop him.

More importantly, no one should try.

"What happened last night?"

"I went on a night hike and fell in a ditch. I'm an idiot."

Hunter scrunched up his brows like he thought maybe Sam had dropped his man card. Poor kid didn't know the half of it. He'd come out of the military at times feeling like less of a man. It wasn't true, of course, and he realized it deep down. He'd been to war with heroes like Tim and Dave who never came back. As for him, he'd simply been privileged to serve alongside them. He certainly had plenty of regrets, but that wasn't one of them.

"Sometimes I do stupid shit. I guess I'll always be a jarhead at heart." Sam took a gulp of hot coffee. "I know why you're here. Ask me anything about the Marine Corps and I'll tell you the honest truth. But be sure you're ready to hear it."

Chapter Eighteen

That evening, Jill went home to Shakira. Sam had listened and stayed—mostly—off his feet all day, supervising with the assistance of a pair of crutches, and later helping her on the spreadsheets. He didn't seem to hate them with quite as much intensity as Jill did. Interestingly, when she'd taken a look at his work she'd been shocked by the suggestions he'd made. He'd found a way to shave off 10 percent from their expenses so that the investors would be even happier. She had no idea they taught this kind of thing in the Marines.

When she'd left the ridge, the guys were all sitting around a campfire, Sam at the center. They seemed to be exchanging war stories, if that was still a thing. She figured she should let them all hang out together in their own little tribe. She'd sort of been monopolizing a lot of Sam's time lately. Giving no hint as to which of them was her favorite, she said goodnight to them all. Sam tipped his beer bottle in her direction and gave her a sly wink.

Yeah, he knew.

Oh, sigh. He really was her favorite. She didn't know what they would do about that, exactly, since sneaking around wasn't really going to work for her. After their grand opening they'd have to come clean with everyone. Because this wasn't going away. Not anytime soon.

"Hello, Shak." Jill checked on her food and water and let her out of the cage. She classically hopped under the table to hide from the world.

Grabbing a glass of wine, Jill opened up her laptop and went to Wildfire Ridge's Facebook profile page. Just another task of many she'd been neglecting. To be funny, she posted status updates on the park as if the park were the one speaking.

The guides are having fun on my lake today. I decided to let them.

But sooner rather than later, Wildfire Ridge should have its own business page so she could run sponsored ads. So not only did she need to hire a general manager, she wanted someone else to maintain all the social media pages. So far all she'd really done was give pithy updates about opening day and upload photos of the ridge, and of the guides.

She uploaded some more photos of the lake, Sam and Julian wakeboarding. Shirtless. She typed:

Our guides, Sam Hawker and Julian Martinez, out on my lake.

Because she'd recently followed all the guides' profiles since Wildfire Ridge needed all the friends it could get, she noticed that Sam's and Julian's names were tagged. She went to their Facebook pages. Sam's was inactive, no surprise, with a photo of a Harley as his profile picture. No status updates, the last photo four years ago, one of a group of friends out on the town. Sam looked happy and carefree, smiling around a cigar as though he was celebrating a special occasion, surrounded by his buddies. He'd also been tagged in that photo, which had come from a profile page of someone by the name of Tim Fischer.

Unable to stop her snooping, she checked his friends list and found a Janet Hawker, with salt-and-pepper hair and familiar blue eyes. She was a professor of Mathematics at Berkeley. He hadn't mentioned that.

The irony wasn't lost on Jill. Both she and Sam came from a family of academics. Maybe they'd both disappointed parents who expected something different out of their children than what they'd received.

Jill understood why his parents had been disappointed in his choice, considering they'd probably given him every opportunity and surrounded him with affluence. They'd likely expected a lot more out of him. University. Graduate school. Maybe even a PhD program. She couldn't imagine Sam behind a desk. He seemed happiest to her on his Harley, hiking, or on a board.

Going back to the Wildfire Ridge page and deciding she'd snooped enough, Jill went back to add more details to the grand opening, making sure the time, date and location were front and center.

See you there!

She added a photo of Sam smiling on the first day he'd climbed the rock.

One week. She couldn't wait.

Sam was beginning to feel a whole lot better about the social thing. Slowly, he'd started to feel human again and not just around Jill. The past couple of nights, he'd sat around the fire pit with the guys. Taking it easy, a foreign concept to him. Not just listening, but talking here and there. Contributing. They talked about the Silver Saddle.

Julian talked about Zoey, whom he was going to take out on a date. They all discussed what a great boss Jill had turned out to be, even if they'd had their doubts in the beginning. All discussed their plans for the foreseeable future. Ty and Julian were going to stick around and stay guides for as long as Jill wanted them. Michael was less sure, since he had an old girlfriend in Los Angeles he wanted to look up.

As for Sam, he had decided he should probably hand in his notice and look for another job in the area. Jill had given him more than a few reasons. She didn't want their connection to end and neither did Sam. While he still didn't think he was at the point where he could be one half of a fully committed partnership, he wanted that with her. He had accepted that if she thought he was good enough for her, he wasn't going to object anymore.

And he was proud of the way he'd handled Hunter's questions about the US Marine Corps. Sam was finally able to separate the expectations from the painful realities and still share some hard-won truths. In the end, he'd never call what they'd all been through together a waste. Having been a Marine and part of a tribe of men he still regarded as brothers remained the single most significant experience of his life. It would never leave him. There was both pain and joy in that reality. No easy answers.

Thing is, he thought maybe he'd finally moved on. Reminders of that old life were in his rearview mirror. The rest of his life stretched out in front of him and now he saw real possibilities. Someday maybe marriage, and hell, even fatherhood. He couldn't help but think that Tim and Dave would be proud.

Wow, what a sap he'd become.

On opening day, he thoroughly enjoyed taking in the sight of the tall redhead who had made him a first-rate sap in no time. Or it might seem that way to most, but considering she'd unknowingly spent an entire year in a medical rehabilitation center with him, if only in his dreams, maybe not.

"Are we ready for this?" She smiled at her staff.

That would be a *hell, yeah*. He and every man here would be willing to die for her if she simply asked. She wouldn't.

The fanfare started off with a ribbon cutting ceremony that included the town mayor, several city council members and of course the Sheriff in attendance. There were several excursions scheduled for the day. Hiking, rock climbing, zip-lining and wakeboarding.

Hunter had come with a few of his friends and the kid was no slouch on the rock climbing wall. He'd make a fine Marine if that was the way he chose to go. It would be his decision, and he'd have to own it. If nothing else, Sam had made that abundantly clear.

Make your own decisions. Live with them. Don't blame anyone else. Never look back.

He was a work in progress.

Sam had just finished checking on a group headed on a five-mile hike and went back toward his trailer after depositing them with Michael, when he saw a familiar-looking woman standing off to the side. She looked extremely out of place, like someone had plucked her out of her life and set her down in this one. All wrong.

His mother.

She walked up to him, staring in disbelief at the boot on his leg. "Are you hurt again?"

Christ, the last thing he needed. A flesh and blood reminder of the life he'd left behind just when he'd finally moved on. He couldn't speak for several minutes, noticing how much older she looked. Her brown hair was salt-and-pepper gray, the lines around her eyes and the deep worry groove between her brows more pronounced. For years, it made her look constantly angry. With him. With the world.

"Hairline fracture. No big deal."

"Other than the crutches, you look amazing. One would never know you spent a year unable to walk at all." She took a step closer.

He closed his eyes and pinched the bridge of his nose. "Why are you here?"

"I didn't think we'd come, and your father...well, he's having a tough time dealing with the idea."

"The idea of my working here?"

"No. The idea that you're home and you didn't tell us." He scowled. "How *is* Dad?"

"He's healthy, if that's what you mean. Takes blood pressure medication, but then so do I. We're getting old."

He'd noticed. The knowledge of how much time they'd been apart sliced through him. Both guilt and resentment hit him at once, like two kicks to the gut. It was his fault. He should have come home on leave to see them again. Should have been more forgiving and all that crap. Instead, he was a stubborn mule of a Marine who didn't want to admit he'd been wrong. Not to them. He hadn't been invincible. Hadn't been untouchable. Hadn't been enough of anything.

"You shouldn't have come."

"Sam, you have to understand. We didn't want you to get hurt. Our biggest fear for you was exactly what happened."

"That sounds a lot like 'I told you so.'"

"No. That's...that's not what I meant." She shook her head, but he got it.

Because she was right and he hated that.

This is where he got to tell her that she was the one who had been right, not him, but the words wouldn't form. Maybe his jaw was too tight. His parents had only wanted to protect him from his somewhat-idealized version of war. Because though they hadn't experienced it themselves, they were well-read professors who understood history far better than he did at the time. And history did tend to repeat itself. At the time, he couldn't imagine what two professors could possibly know about the military.

And he'd wanted to make his own way. Find his own path.

True, there was much they'd been clueless about. But if he'd listened to even half of what they tried to tell him, maybe he'd have at least been better prepared. Eyes wide-open. In the end, it wouldn't have changed the outcome. No one would have stopped him and no one should have tried. He'd found his tribe, and he'd never regret the time he spent with his brothers both dead and alive. It hadn't been a waste because in the end he hadn't fought for the overall mission, but for the man standing beside him.

"I'm kind of in the middle of something," Sam ground out. "Working."

She stepped away. "I won't bother you anymore."

He wondered if she realized he could have gone anywhere in the United States. But he'd come back home. He hadn't overanalyzed that bit. There was usually plenty of work in California and it made sense to land here. But maybe he'd come back to punish himself. With reminders all around him of who he'd been when he left and who he was now. Not the same man. That much was certain.

He watched her go, a rush of emotions hitting him at once. Regret. Pain. He'd lost too much in his life. It seemed he'd never get to keep something, or someone.

Chapter Nineteen

Something was wrong. It was clear in every strained angle of Sam's tight jawline. But Jill couldn't imagine what had gone wrong. The day had progressed exactly as planned. No accidents. No clients regretting their choice of activity and backing out at the last minute. Most were a bunch of athletes looking for their next fix. There were a few older teens like Hunter, who'd come with a group of friends. Everyone seemed happy and satisfied with the experience.

But Sam kept avoiding Jill, and when they ran into each other he wouldn't look at her.

At the end of a successful opening day, Jill gathered the troops and offered to pay for dinner. Pizza on her tab.

"I'm good." Sam excused himself and retired to his trailer.

"Extra large with pepperoni and sausage," Julian said. "And whatever these two bozos want."

"Good one!" Ty said, and both he and Michael grabbed Julian in a headlock.

Sighing that boys would be boys, Jill let them wrestle each other to the ground while she ordered two extra-large pizzas and threw glances in the direction of Sam's trailer.

Once the pizzas had been delivered and Jill paid for them, she took a slice and made small talk with the men. She hadn't paid any one of them even half the attention she had Sam.

Michael brought a few beers out from his trailer to share. "Should we shower our fearless leader in cold beer, or does someone have a Gatorade?"

"In your dreams, guys. In your dreams."

She stayed for a while longer, but couldn't stop thinking about Sam in his trailer alone. Would it be too obvious if she joined him now? Just to check on him? Surely the guys would understand. Maybe something about today had brought back an old memory that he would now be trying to shake off.

When the men were deeply immersed in a conversation on whether the Giants had the best pitcher in the league this year or if the guy was a chump, Jill casually excused herself. She rapped on Sam's trailer door but let herself in without waiting for him to open it.

She found him leaning against the kitchen counter, nursing a beer, staring in the direction of his door.

"Come on in," he said through hooded eyes.

She supposed that was a dig on the fact that she hadn't waited for an invitation. "What's wrong?"

He took one last gulp of his beer and set the bottle down. "Nothing."

Lie number one. He had the same off-putting dangerous look of the first night she met him. Everything in him shouted "stay away" and she was transported back to that night. A night when she'd had the courage of someone who had nothing invested. Nothing to lose. Amazing how easy it had been for her to make a move with little on the line. Now she had everything to risk and her fear was in this room with them, large and stifling enough to make it hard to breathe.

"Sam, come on."

"What."

His tone was clipped. Annoyed.

"Something happened today. What was it?"

He'd made such progress that he was almost a different man from the one she'd first met. Lighter. But now he was right back to square one and she had no idea why.

"I came to my senses, that's what happened. This thing between us is not working. I'm moving on."

She could feel the anger and hostility dripping off him. The intensity of his heat, not a good one this time, had her hand shaking and lowering to her side. She'd never imagined it would end this way when they'd gotten past all the baggage Sam carried with him.

But she got that maybe this was something Sam would never get past.

"Moving on?"

"Leaving Fortune. I thought I could do this, thought I could stay and be with you but I can't."

"Why?" She took a deep and quivering breath. "I need you, Sam."

"You only think you do."

"What happened?"

"I saw a flesh and blood reminder of who I *used* to be. You would have really liked that guy. He believed in the cause. He was patriotic. Invincible. He didn't think he could ever lose. He would have died for his country and for his friends. Instead, they died for him. Is that what you want to hear?"

There was so much raw pain in his voice that it shot straight through her and she shook at the wall of suffering radiating from him. She could sense every ounce of agony pouring through him and wondered how she could have missed it before.

Survivor's guilt.

Also known as the wound that never healed. The battle that never ended.

He turned his back to her.

"I didn't…kn-know." Her voice trembled and she could only hear the pounding of her heartbeat.

"Didn't want you to know. Some things should never be discussed."

"No, Sam." She bit back tears and spoke past the stone in her throat. "They do need to be discussed. It isn't anyone's fault and it might help to talk about it."

"No," he ground out between clenched teeth.

"Not to *me*. You need help."

"And I remember telling you I don't need your help."

"You went through a rough time and you lived through it, which isn't anything to be ashamed about. It's a second chance."

He turned but wouldn't meet her eyes. "You'll have my resignation by tomorrow."

"You're leaving? Just like that?"

"I'll stay until you find someone else to take my place. I'm sure there are plenty of men from Home at Last who need a job. Last I heard there was a waiting list for this place."

What about us, she wanted to ask, because now they could really be together. But she understood the truth in his clipped words. The love she had discovered, that deep connection with him that went beyond the physical, wasn't reciprocated. Either that, or Sam was no longer capable of connecting with anyone on any level. He was too damaged. Too filled with guilt and remorse that he refused to let go.

"But I don't want you to go."

"Look, babe, our one-night stand is now about a month too long. We should have called it a day after the second time. Maybe we pushed our luck."

The fresh and solid pain he'd meant to bring didn't fail to hit her like a punch to the throat.

"Sure," she said, using every bit of the courage he'd shown her that she had. "Maybe we did."

"No hard feelings."

"Not at all." She tossed her hair and blinked the tears back. "I had fun."

Then she turned and opened the door to his trailer. Shut it without a second look back. The guys had retired to their trailers, or were hiding somewhere. Maybe they'd heard. Maybe they knew she'd made a fool out of herself by falling for one of her guides.

What a joke she was. Hoping for love and looking for it in a man who would never be available to her. Which meant as far as she'd come, she still hadn't learned a damned thing.

Pushing back tears with the pads of her fingers, she hopped in her truck and drove down the hill on her way home.

When Sam heard the sound of a knock on his door a few minutes later, he braced for impact, hoping it wasn't Jill. Because if she walked through that door again without waiting for an invitation, he would not only ravage her but tell her that he wasn't going to ever be able to let her go. Her parting words to him had been said in a trembling voice, and her eyes told him one story, while her gentle words let him go. The courage she displayed in the simple letting go shocked him to the core. No sobbing. No angry recriminations.

She thought this was what he wanted. What he needed. And she was willing to give it to him. She was amazing. Beautiful and courageous and a hell of a warrior even if she didn't know that. It didn't hurt that she'd nailed it. Yes, he needed help. Help he hadn't received by blaming or driving himself physically to the point of exhaustion.

Christ, he was so tired.

When Sam opened the door, it was Julian on the other side. "Hey."

"What's up?" He put some edge in his tone, hoping Julian would walk away without prying.

But no such luck. Julian shoved past Sam. "Sorry about Jill."

"What? You heard?" He didn't think either of them had been loud.

"I wasn't 100 percent sure until just now." He grinned. "But yeah, we didn't miss that she came in here and then took off like demons had chased her away."

No demons. Just him, and that was bad enough. As he feared he would, he'd hurt her. But he hadn't ruined her. She was strong and would recover from this.

He wasn't certain he ever would, but that wasn't the point.

Now he'd risked her reputation, too. He shoved a hand down his face. "We were that obvious. How long have you known?"

"Dude, since day one. We just weren't going to say anything. Your secret is safe with us."

"It's complicated. I actually met her a while back. Before she hired me."

"You're a lucky man."

"Thanks, but it's over." He moved to the fridge and offered Julian a cold one. "I'm moving on as soon as she finds a replacement."

"She *dumped* you?"

Dump. There was a word. Sam grimaced. "I need to get on to the next job. Maybe go to Colorado."

"But this is a great gig. You love it here."

"It's time to go."

"Hell, no. It isn't."

Sam quirked a brow.

"It's time to face it, whatever *it* is. Whatever you're dealing with, it's going to go with you. Time to stop running and just let it happen. Here or wherever you go next, it's never leaving you until you let it go."

"What do you know about it?"

"Listen, remember that I was there, too. Maybe not a hard-ass Marine but you know I saw…things. I thought I'd never stop replaying the tape over and over in my mind. But one day it got better. It's never going away but it gets to a point where you can deal with it." He locked gazes with Sam. "Been to the VA?"

Sam knew exactly what he meant. "Once."

And then he'd figured out that talking didn't help. He didn't want to be medicated. The only thing that helped was to keep moving and find the hardest and most physically challenging thing he could. Except that he'd proved there wasn't anything strenuous or tough enough to make him forget.

There also wasn't a woman sweet and brave enough to help him. He'd proved that. Which meant he was SOL.

"Go again," Julian said, brooking no argument. "And again."

"Look—"

Julian held up a palm. "No bullshit. I've been there, done that. I'm no better than you are and if I can move on, so can you. We already gave *enough*. Maybe not as much as some of our friends, but that wasn't our choice. So we have to give our best effort to whatever we've got left now, and for the rest of our lives. I've got a lot of friends' memories to honor and I'm sure you do, too."

"Yeah."

"Don't be a jerk. Go get yourself another job, get your act together and go get that woman back. She is cuckoo for Cocoa Puffs crazy about you."

Sam didn't know why it was so much harder for him. He'd seen many of his friends move on and get past their time in the service. Jobs in law enforcement and as first responders. If he'd had his head screwed on straight, he might have tried to do the same. Why couldn't he move on? Unless Jill was right and he had to reconcile with the past he'd never be able to leave behind.

After a few minutes more of sitting quietly with each other, drinking, words seemingly no longer necessary, Julian said good-night and left.

It occurred to Sam that for one tough Marine, he'd been afraid of two people who never meant to hurt him. He'd avoided them, which had him at an impasse. Because he could almost physically feel the hurt and pain he'd caused them and it was just one more responsibility he couldn't shoulder.

Tomorrow morning his first phone call would be to the VA. But as he picked up his phone now, he dialed a number he'd never forgotten. If talking could make him whole again and deserving of one little spitfire named Jill Davis, he would face it no matter what it took from him.

When his mother answered on the first ring, he simply said, "Hey, thanks for coming today."

And after all this time, at least it was a beginning.

Chapter Twenty

Jill didn't get upset when she got home and realized that she hadn't shut Shakira's cage securely enough. She'd crashed through it and left a little bunny trail of dark pellets from one end of the house to the other. Well, that was Jill's fault. She also didn't get upset that Shak had found her way into the bathroom and shredded through several rolls of toilet paper. Also her fault for leaving them out where Shak could get to them. She cleaned up the messes, fed Shak and went to her cupboard for her chocolate stash. Nothing there, so she went to her emergency stash. The one she kept hidden under the sink.

And it was all gone.

"C'mon! I haven't been eating *that* much chocolate. How could this happen? Why me?"

She wanted to shake her fist toward the heavens but instead burst into tears. Shakira stopped munching on her food long enough to stare vacantly into space. It was almost as if she was saying: "Woman, if you're going to be that dramatic, at least take acting lessons first. You're horrible!"

If she had a dog or a cat, the pet would curl up into Jill's lap and make her feel loved and needed. Valued. Unconditional love. That's what she'd wanted all her life. From her parents. Her brother. From her friends. From the men she'd dated. From her pets! But all she had was Shak who, though very cute—let's face it—seemed completely clueless to Jill's pain.

Jill dialed Zoey. "Do you have chocolate?"

"Of course I have chocolate. What's wrong?"

"I'm all out and this is an emergency."

"I'll be right over."

Five minutes later, Zoey was at Jill's carrying a paper bag in one hand and Boo's leash in the other. "Reinforcements have arrived."

Jill folded into Zoey's arms. "I want a dog! I need a dog."

"And it sounds like you're finally ready."

"Really?" She sniffed. "I think so, too."

"What about Boo? He still needs a home and I'd trust you with him in a heartbeat."

Boo was nearly the size of a horse, her kindred animal. "I don't think my place is large enough."

Zoey sighed. "I guess you're right."

"You'll be on the lookout for me?"

"Of course. I'll find you the perfect dog. Someone loyal and well trained who just wants to love on you."

Oh my, that sounded good. Jill took the bag from Zoey and plunked down on the couch, digging in.

Zoey sat beside her, parking Boo nearby. "What about a nice lap dog?"

"I was actually thinking a Lab."

Zoey deadpanned. "A Lab. They're kind of big, too."

Jill burst into tears. Again. "I could handle it."

"Oh, I'm sorry. I didn't mean it. Of course you can adopt a Lab." Zoey flew into fix-it mode. "Why not? I mean if you take it to work with you it would have loads of room."

That didn't make Jill feel any better. She'd have a Labrador but no Sam. And a Lab, beautiful though they were, couldn't replace Sam. After a few minutes, Jill explained everything to Zoey between her stupid hiccuping and tears.

The blurred lines in the workplace between her and Sam. The time they'd spent together. All she'd learned about him.

Lastly, the worst news of all. "I fell in love."

"I know you did." Zoey sniffed, sympathy tears glistening in her dark brown lashes. "You can't help who you love."

"I screwed up, Z. I should have never slept with him again."

"You didn't screw up. What's wrong with taking a chance on love?"

"Making a damn fool out of myself when I knew better."

"No." Zoey shook her head. "I've been your friend for years and never seen you as happy as these past weeks. Sam came back into your life for a reason. He changed you. For years, all you cared about was your career and making a big splash in the world. You dated men but never got attached, probably because you wouldn't let yourself. But when Sam came along all the rules changed. I think only love can do that. And you can't waste time regretting love."

Jill sniffed. "He resigned, and now I have to work with him until I find a replacement. I have to see him every day and know that he doesn't feel the same way. He was fooling around and I was falling in love."

"Typical man."

"No. Not typical at all. He's hurting. He needs help, and I don't know if he'll get it."

Zoey nodded sadly and glanced toward a calm Boo, sitting regally as he observed two women drown in chocolate. "It hurts too much to let anyone near even if all you want to do is help."

Jill and Zoey sat in a sea of chocolate wrappers, and by the time Zoey left, Jill felt a tiny bit better. So she'd made mistakes before. Trusted people she shouldn't have. This one hurt more than anything before, but then she'd been the one to get her heart involved.

But she'd learned one thing she'd never before suspected. Sam was correct. She was brave and it was high time she acknowledged it to herself.

For a long time, she'd simply wanted to make Ryan and her parents proud. But she had to be happy, too.

Jill had never been a parent, so she couldn't imagine what it was like to have a child who was very ill. She had to assume that it would be hard to let go. Hard not to expect more bad news coming. But they hadn't given her enough credit. She was a hell of a fighter and Sam had taught her to understand that. It might be that her family would never stop seeing her as a sickly girl, but the important thing was that Jill knew she was much more than that.

A sense of relief flooded her, knowing she'd crossed one more item off her unwritten list. There were some things she'd never write on a list, since they might never happen. She'd been smart for many years and only written down measurable goals she could achieve. But she'd never written down some of the stuff she really wanted out of life over which she had little control.

Fall in love with a wonderful man. Have two point three children. Adopt a dog.

That last one was easy considering she had an in with the dog lady. She'd just been waiting to be ready for so many things. Like permanent love. And a dog. Remembering how Sam had called Zoey "the dog lady" and looked mortified after he had brought about a new wave of pain and regret. He'd seemed a bit like a lost soul the first time she'd met him. A sexy, brooding lost man she didn't want to know for longer than a few uninterrupted hours.

Who knew that would flip on a dime and he'd be the one to crack open her heart and then break it?

For two weeks, Jill went home every afternoon to Shakira. Sam, of course, had a gift for disappearing about the time Jill arrived for work every morning. And he'd been leaving two to three times a week like clockwork at the end of his day. She had no idea whether or not he came back to the trailer or if he'd already met someone new he was spending his nights alongside. Best not to know. Julian and Ty gave her sympathetic looks from time to time, which meant they must know everything. Michael, for his part, seemed oblivious. But, hey, as long as she held her head up high and didn't cop to it, she could pretend she and Sam were an overblown rumor.

She'd recently hired both a receptionist and scheduler. Audrey stayed in Jill's old trailer, which they both shared during the day as an office and Audrey had to herself at night. Jill had replaced the cot. She'd also hired a social media manager who worked off-site. Three more guides from Home at Last would start next week. Even if Sam decided to stay after all, she would need more men. She reported to her investors on their grand opening and the schedule booked six months in advance, and the consensus of the board remained that she should hire a general manager to report to the board. No amount of persuasion seemed to convince them otherwise. There was now more than a budget for a general manager, who would work side by side with her as CEO. A budget, but no one she wanted to hire yet.

Not anyone who would stick around.

Near the end of the week, Julian pulled Jill aside. "How you doing, boss?"

She gripped her clipboard harder. Never went anywhere without it these days. "Good, good. Everything's shipshape around here."

"Shipshape?" Julian seemed to be trying to choke back a laugh. "He's doing good, too. Wanted you to know."

"That's great. I'm glad."

He probably already had another girlfriend and the decency not to throw it in her face. And so did Julian.

"I should have a replacement for him soon. You can tell him that."

"Why don't you?"

"Oh sure. I will next time I see him." And since they were avoiding each other, that could be a while.

Julian tipped an imaginary hat and walked away grinning.

She would be okay. Eventually. All the delegating Sam had convinced her was important had allowed her some free time. She hadn't quite known what to do with herself at first, but then she'd learned to relax again. A foreign concept. She'd had dinner with her parents once they'd returned from Paris. They'd acted pleased about the success of the park, which meant that, god bless them, they were trying. She'd started biking again. Attended a few barbecues at Carly and Levi's home with their large group of friends. All the things normal people did who had regular and balanced lives.

If there was a hole in her heart, she'd get over it someday. She didn't have any regrets, just as she'd told Sam. No regrets about San Francisco and no regrets about what he'd termed their "month-long one-night stand." The important thing was that she'd risked her heart for the first time. She'd learned her heart was big enough to love someone deeply enough to let him go. He'd needed her to let him go and she'd made it easy for him because he deserved getting whatever he wanted for once.

Finally, her week at an end, Jill was late to work the next morning. She'd taken her time, letting Shakira out in the backyard to have a grass party and then having to spend an hour trying to get her back in the house, chasing her as she hopped from one shrub to another. Turned out rabbits were fast.

Live and learn.

As she crossed the entrance, the American flag waving in the light summer breeze, she slowed when she noticed Sam standing near the flagpole on his crutches. Alone.

A memory hit her hard and fast of the first time they'd met as Jill and Sam, not *Angelina and Chris*. It was a short time ago but seemed longer. They'd both changed so much when they dropped their masks and their fake names. Much of that change had hurt. Then again, she should have expected a few growing pains.

When he moved to block her car from going any farther, she stopped and got out.

"What's going on?"

"I want to talk to you and it has to be away from everyone else."

"Sorry." She dipped her head. "They already know."

"But they don't have to know *everything*. Some of this is private." He took her hand and tugged her into his arms.

"Sam?" Her heart cracked opened. She was afraid to say another word.

"I haven't told you everything and I should have. You don't know this but you saved me, girl. I might have been in a hell of a mood the night we first met, but I had no idea what was coming next. The toughest year of my life. When I was in that medical facility going through PT and hoping one day I'd walk again, it was your face that I saw. You were my lifeline and didn't even know it. Because you were the last time I felt normal. The last time I felt alive."

"Oh, Sam. Why didn't you tell me?" She buried her face in his neck.

"I've been really bitter for a long time. When I saw you again, it was like getting a second chance. I was afraid I'd blow that chance, too. And I almost did because I'm so pissed off at myself and the world." He took a deep breath and pressed his forehead to hers as his words caught. "I'm getting help because I know I need it."

"That's where you've been going every other afternoon? I thought…"

"What?"

"That maybe you had a new girlfriend."

He tipped her chin in his hand and went brows up. "Seriously? No, Boots. There's no other woman on this planet for me. No one else has my back like you do. Say you'll give this jarhead another chance."

"I will. You mean everything to me and I don't want to lose you ever."

"No, I think you're stuck with me. Forever, if you'll have me. I love you, Jill."

The thought sent a thrill up her spine. "I love you

so much. But there's something you still need to know about me."

"Yeah?" Palming her neck, he studied her carefully.

"Zoey says my kindred animal is a horse."

"Ah," he said, grinning. "Is that any better than having a cat as a kindred animal?"

"Probably not." She went up on tiptoe and smiled against his lips. "Maybe we could meet in the middle with a—"

"Lab," they both said at once.

He laughed and kissed her, long and hard, squeezing her so tightly she thought she might burst.

When she came up for air, she said, "I have some bad news. You're fired."

He had the decency to look disappointed. "I'd rather look for another job than lose you."

"How do you feel about a general manager position? Because the board of investors is insisting someone be hired. You'd be reporting to them. Not me."

"Shame. I sort of liked reporting to you." He grinned and tugged her in tighter.

"Well, I'm sure we could do a little of that here and there."

"Promise?"

"Yes, promise. Sam Hawker, will you please do me the honor of being our general manager and making me the happiest CEO in the world?"

"Jill Davis, try and stop me."

Epilogue

One month later

"Fubar!" Jill shouted for the full-grown Labrador and Golden mix she'd adopted almost a month ago through Paws n Pilots.

Granted, he was well trained, but for a three-legged dog he moved fast. He also had a lot of room to roam on the ridge and Jill didn't want to lose sight of him. But as she walked up a hill to her future home, she wasn't surprised to find Fubar inside the frame of her unfinished home.

She and Sam were now living in his trailer together, and had leased the land from Wildfire Ridge's Outdoor Adventures. The company was doing much better than even she could have expected, and Sam was building their home on the top of the hill. From here, they would have a view of the entire ridge.

She stepped through the frame of the house, bent to pet Fubar and followed the pounding. She found Sam on a ladder in what would be their kitchen eventually. He was shirt-less, wore a pair of faded jeans, a tool belt around his slim hips, and a nail between his teeth. She'd seriously never seen anything sexier in her life. And she'd seen Sam all soaped up and naked in the shower, so this said something.

Among all his many talents, Sam also knew his way around a construction site and had worked in the field for a while after leaving the service.

"Sam," she said, coming to the bottom of the ladder. "Fubar keeps following you in here."

Not that she blamed the dog. Who wouldn't follow Sam? But he didn't want Fubar in here, worried he'd step on a nail.

"Hey, boy." Sam came down the ladder. "Guess we're going to have to go over 'stay' again."

"Aw, you can't blame him. He wants to be with you. So do I, by the way."

He quirked a brow. "You're with me every night."

"And your point is…?"

"Not sick of me yet?" He winked.

"Never. But it is getting pretty cramped in the trailer especially with Fubar and Shakira. And as much as I love sleeping on top of you, I can't wait to get a nice big bedroom that's not part of the kitchen. When will our bedroom be ready again?" She batted her eyelashes.

As it happened, she asked this question once a day, but Sam didn't seem to mind.

"As soon as your state-of-the-art kitchen is ready. Walls go up next week." He tugged on her hand, and led her toward the back of the house. "Let me show you something."

As she walked through their home, her diamond ring caught a sunbeam through the roofless house. Sam had surprised her and bought her a ring with his signing bonus for coming on as general manager. Their engagement had seemed fast to everyone, including their parents, but Jill had never been more certain in her life. She was in this life with Sam, come whatever. Forever.

She stood in the frame of the bedroom, near a large opening facing the lake.

"This is going to be our picture window. Check out the view from here. On a good day, you can see clear into the valley."

The view was incredible. Acres of trees, the pristine lake and the rugged landscape of the ridge. Last week a family of deer had been spotted in the area. This was the direction Sam had taken on the hike where he'd been injured.

This was where they'd have their wedding day. Right here on Wildfire Ridge.

"It's beautiful. But also, there's a mountain lion out there that wants to have us for dinner."

He chuckled, pulled her into his arms and spoke into her hair. "Boots, you never have to worry about being eaten by a mountain lion. Remember you have your own lion right here."

She framed his face. "Baby, your kindred animal was a *cat*."

"A big cat." He gave her his boyish grin.

"Cat, big cat or lion I really don't care. The important thing is that you're mine."

"I always will be. Always."

* * * * *

*Look for the next book in the
Wildfire Ridge miniseries,
coming in January 2020!*

*And for more great romances by Heatherly Bell,
try the Heroes of Fortune Valley miniseries:*

Breaking Emily's Rules
Airman to the Rescue
This Baby Business

Available now!

*And if you're looking for more military romance,
check out these great books from
Harlequin Special Edition:*

Having the Soldier's Baby
By Tara Taylor Quinn

His Baby Bargain
By Cathy Gillen Thacker

The SEAL's Secret Daughter
By Christy Jeffries

*To give the orphaned triplets they're guardians of the
stability they need, Lulu McCabe and Sam Kirkland
decide to jointly adopt them. But when it's discovered
their marriage wasn't actually annulled, they have
to prove to the courts they're responsible—
by renewing their vows!*

Read on for a sneak preview of Cathy Gillen Thacker's
Their Inherited Triplets,
*the next book in the
Texas Legends: The McCabes miniseries.*

"The two of you are still married," Liz said.

"Still?" Lulu croaked.

Sam asked, "What are you talking about?"

"More to the point, how do you know this?" Lulu
demanded, the news continuing to hit her like a gut punch.

Travis looked down at the papers in front of him.
"Official state records show you eloped in the Double
Knot Wedding Chapel in Memphis, Tennessee, on
Monday, March 14, nearly ten years ago. Alongside
another couple, Peter and Theresa Thompson, in a double
wedding ceremony."

Lulu gulped. "But our union was never legal," she
pointed out, trying to stay calm, while Sam sat beside her
in stoic silence.

Liz countered, "Ah, actually, it is legal. In fact, it's still
valid to this day."

Sam reached over and took her hand in his, much as he had the first time they had been in this room together. "How is that possible?" Lulu asked weakly.

"We never mailed in the certificate of marriage, along with the license, to the state of Tennessee," Sam said.

"And for our union to be recorded and therefore legal, we had to have done that," Lulu reiterated.

"Well, apparently, the owners of the Double Knot Wedding Chapel did, and your marriage was recorded. And is still valid to this day, near as we can tell. Unless you two got a divorce or an annulment somewhere else? Say another country?" Travis prodded.

"Why would we do that? We didn't know we were married," Sam returned.

Don't miss
Their Inherited Triplets *by Cathy Gillen Thacker,*
available August 2019 wherever
Harlequin® Special Edition books and ebooks are sold.

www.Harlequin.com

*Read on for a sneak peek at
the first funny and heart-tugging book in Jo McNally's
Rendezvous Falls series,* Slow Dancing at Sunrise!

"I'd have thought the idea of me getting caught in a rainstorm would make your day."

He gave her a quick glance. Just because she was off-limits didn't mean he was blind.

"Trust me, it did." Luke slowed the truck and reached behind the seat to grab his zippered hoodie hanging there. Whitney looked down and her cheeks flamed when she realized how her clothes were clinging to her. She snatched the hoodie from his hand before he could give it to her, and thrust her arms into it without offering any thanks. Even the zipper sounded pissed off when she yanked it closed.

"Perfect. Another guy with more testosterone than manners. Nice to know it's not just a Chicago thing. Jackasses are everywhere."

Luke frowned. He'd been having fun at her expense, figuring she'd give it right back to him as she had before. But her words hinted at a story that didn't reflect well on men in general. She'd been hurt. He shouldn't care. But that quick dimming of the fight in her eyes made him feel ashamed. *That* was a new experience.

A flash of lightning made her flinch. But the thunder didn't follow as quickly as the last time. The storm was moving off. He drove from the vineyard into the parking lot and over to the main house. The sound of the rain on the roof was less angry. But Whitney wasn't. She was clutching his sweatshirt around herself, her knuckles white. From anger? Embarrassment? Both? Luke shook his head.

"Look, I thought I was doing the right thing, driving up there." He rubbed the back of his neck and grimaced, remembering how sweaty and filthy he still was. "It's not my fault you walked out of the woods soaking wet. I mean, I try not to be a jackass, but I'm still a man. And I *did* offer my hoodie."

Whitney's chin pointed up toward the second floor of the main house. Her neck was long and graceful. There was a vein pulsing at the base of it. She blinked a few times, and for a horrifying moment, he thought there might be tears shimmering there in her eyes. *Damn it.* The last thing he needed was to have Helen's niece *crying* in his truck. He opened his mouth to say something—anything—but she beat him to it.

"I'll concede I wasn't prepared for rain." Her mouth barely moved, her words forced through clenched teeth. "But a gentleman would have looked away or…something."

His low laughter was enough to crack that brittle shell of hers. She turned to face him, eyes wide.

"See, Whitney, that's where you made your biggest mistake." He shrugged. "It wasn't going out for a day hike with a storm coming." He talked over her attempted objection. "Your *biggest* mistake was thinking I'm any kind of gentleman."

The corner of her mouth tipped up into an almost smile. "But you said you weren't a jackass."

"There's a hell of a lot of real estate between jackass and gentleman, babe."

Her half smile faltered, then returned. That familiar spark appeared in her eyes. The crack in her veneer had been repaired, and the sharp edge returned to her voice. Any other guy might have been annoyed, but Luke was oddly relieved to see Whitney back in fighting form.

"The fact that you just referred to me as 'babe' tells me you're a lot closer to jackass than you think."

He lifted his shoulder. "I never told you which end of the spectrum I fell on."

The rain had slowed to a steady drizzle. She reached for the door handle, looking over her shoulder with a smirk.

"Actually, I'm pretty sure you just did."

She hurried up the steps to the covered porch. He waited, but she didn't look back before going into the house. Her energy still filled the cab of the truck, and so did her scent. Spicy, woodsy, rain soaked. Finally coming to his senses, he threw the truck into Reverse and headed back toward the carriage house. He needed a long shower. A long *cold* one.

Don't miss
Jo McNally's Slow Dancing at Sunrise,
available July 2019 from HQN Books!

www.Harlequin.com